To Mary

Romance and intrigue—a powerful combination—but this isn't the Love Boat. Get ready to be captivated as Donna Dawson's spell-binding thriller, *Vengeance,* puts you on a luxury cruise where the hors d'oeuvre are rounds of heart pounding suspense.

~Keith Clemons, 5X award wining author
of *Angel in the Alley* and *These Little Ones*

God's blessings
Donna Dawson

D0107138

Vengeance

Donna Dawson

VENGEANCE
© 2008 Donna Dawson

ISBN-10: 1-897373-24-4
ISBN-13: 978-1-897373-24-8

All rights reserved. No part of this publication may be reproduced, stored in a retrieval system, or transmitted in any form or by any means—electronic, mechanical, photocopy, recording, or any other—except for brief quotations in printed reviews, without the prior permission of the publisher.

This book is a work of fiction. Names, characters, places, and incidents are the product of the author's imagination or are used fictitiously. Any resemblance to actual events, locales, or persons, living or dead, is coincidental.

All scripture quotations, unless otherwise indicated, are taken from the HOLY BIBLE, NEW INTERNATIONAL VERSION®. NIV®. Copyright ©1973, 1978, 1984 by International Bible Society. Used by permission of Zondervan. All rights reserved.

To contact the author, please email:
authordonnadawson@hotmail.com

WORD ALIVE PRESS

Published by Word Alive Press
131 Cordite Road, Winnipeg, MB R3W 1S1
www.wordalivepress.ca

Table of Contents

Acknowledgements

To my dear mother who fought so bravely against the enemy named cancer and surrendered with dignity and grace only when her Saviour called her home. Her witness in life and in death has had a profound impact and she will be sorely missed.

Thank you to my dearest husband, who encouraged me to keep on when I didn't want to.

Thank you to my families—biological and spiritual—for cheering me on from the sidelines.

Thank you to Caroline Schmidt and Larissa Bartos of Word Alive Press for their patience and excellent work in publishing and editing. Without you, my ministry of writing would have been a long time in coming.

Thank you to The Word Guild for providing an excellent venue for Christian Writers to learn and build friendships.

Thank you to my local writing group. You all challenge me with your gentle but accurate critiques, lift me with your camaraderie and your encouragement and don't allow me to give up.

Thank you to our Saviour, who doesn't give us what we deserve.

Donna Dawson

Vengeance

Sunday, February 4, 2005
San Diego

11:00 am	Start embarkation
12:00 nn	Light breeze. Partly overcast skies, 17°C
5:00 pm	Undocked
5:40 pm	Disembarked local pilot

The sixty-one-thousand-tonne cruise ship *The Cormorant* cut through the Pacific waters with a grace that was surprising for its size. With its diesel engines pushing it inexorably further into the seven-foot waves and its automatic stabilizers engaged, the seven-hundred-and-eighty-foot vessel rocked gently, impervious to the growing choppiness of the ocean.

Twelve hundred eager passengers settled comfortably into their small cabins, happy to begin the journey which would lead them to and from the tropical paradise known as the Hawaiian Islands. Six hundred and fifty crew members drawn from a handful of third world countries were primed and ready to cater to the many needs and wants of the ship's guests. Myriad reasons brought this collection of people together on the all-inclusive floating hotel. It would be a journey that they would not forget.

*The mission of the FBI is to protect and defend the United States against terrorist and foreign intelligence threats, to uphold and enforce the criminal laws of the United States, and to provide leadership and criminal justice services to federal, state, municipal, and international agencies and partners.

---

* FBI website mission statement <u>www.fbi.gov</u>

~Prelude

I T WAS A HARSH LAND. A land created for survivors. Ruggedly beautiful in summer, sharp snow-capped granite peaks jabbed at crisp blue skies, their formidable structures providing a starkly contrasting backdrop. Endless carpets of wildflowers, moss and boldly coloured soil blanketed the vast horizons. And then there were the brutal winters that sealed the land in a tight cocoon of glacial ice, numbing cold and stifling darkness. Far from the eyes of the governing authorities, it was the perfect place to experiment in areas that would otherwise be frowned upon. And it was, after all, only one Beluga whale. Even if the carcass was later found, it would be impossible for anyone to trace the elements back to their source.

The man watched as his subordinate's hand cranked the cable that ran from the small but sturdy crane to the net-encased mammal not thirty feet from the stern of the mid-sized fishing vessel. The boat rocked with the thrashing of the pathetic creature as it heaved its blanched hide in protest of the rough hemp. The erratic jerking and yanking was offset by the hypnotic rhythm of Hudson Bay's stiff tides and currents, and the man was anxious for the thing to be done and over so he could return to the safety of land.

He studied the whale as it was pulled alongside the ship. Alabaster white, it was a beautiful mammal. *Almost a pity to destroy the thing.* But, as seemed to be the norm in this crazy world, it was an innocent in the hands of someone else's agenda. The whale stilled and, as instructed, the men kept it half-submerged. There was no point in stressing it any more than necessary.

He walked to the rail and reached down into a box lined with foam packing materials. Pulling out a large syringe, the man held it up to the grey skies and eyed the dose of clear fluid it contained. It should be enough to give them an accurate testing. If it could kill the whale, it would most certainly do its job on its other intended victims.

He patted the animal's smooth, streamlined skin gently—almost apologetically. And then he plunged the syringe deep, emptying it of its contents. Surprisingly, the creature never moved. Its eyes were just above the waterline and it rolled the nearest one back to fasten on the man with the syringe. As though it knew its own fate. Returning the instrument back to its case, the man settled back to wait. He figured maybe three hours at best and then the creature would begin to show signs.

Ignoring the quiet whale, the man filled the gradual passing of time by scanning the nearby shore, keeping an alert eye out for any human intervention. It would be awkward explaining what had just been done. Better that there were no witnesses. Along a rocky outcropping, a flock of long-tailed ducks waddled and fussed, pleased with the mild summer as they preened their young and themselves. The tundra was vibrant with unusual and persistent life in the short span of time allowed for the warm season.

The man knew all about the tundra. He had studied it in great detail. He knew every plant from the arctic cotton that swayed in the crisp winds to the lousewort and saxifrage that covered the ground in a tenacious blanket. He had followed the migratory paths of the caribou, seen the polar bear in action and felt his heart swell with the aerial ballets danced by the peregrine falcons, snowy owls and Sabine's gulls. This was a land he could truly love, given a different life. But he only had the life he'd been handed and he would make certain it counted for something—in spite of those who had brutally and unknowingly shaped it. Because of them.

He turned his eye back to the Beluga. It had settled into the net after its first violent protest and continued to wait patiently for whatever it was meant to wait for. The creature had earned his instant respect and, again, he felt a twinge of remorse. Glancing at his watch, he was surprised to find that the three hours had come and gone in his fascinated study of the landscape. He moved closer to the seized whale and examined every inch of its sturdy form. Nothing. A frown flickered across his brow and he turned to his associate. "Are you certain the dose was right?"

The smaller, bespectacled man merely shrugged and nodded.

"I wonder what's gone wrong, then." He turned back to the whale and gave it another once-over.

"I don't understand it, sir. This compound is strong enough that it should have shown its mark long before now.

Maybe I should draw a tissue sample and take it back to the lab to see what went wrong."

The man nodded and stepped out of the smaller man's path. "Get it done, then release the poor creature and we'll be off. I'll contact my chopper pilot and he can pick us up on shore. Don't dawdle." He gave his associate a knowing look and reached into his pocket for his two-way radio. "We're ready." He barked the two words into the receiver, waited for acknowledgement, then turned to the vessel's captain. "We'll pick up my chopper on shore. I'll need your lifeboat to get myself and the doctor there. Would that be a problem?"

The ten thousand dollars above the rental fee for the fishing vessel pretty much guaranteed that it likely wouldn't be, and the Captain shrugged his submission.

Finished with his ministrations over the whale, the doctor turned and secured the tissue sample alongside the empty syringe in the padded case. He rose and heaved the bulky case into his arms, almost jealously, and manoeuvred across the open deck to where the lifeboat was being lowered to the water's rolling surface. Before long, the two men were settled, side by side, in the small wooden motor boat and heading for shore.

No one aboard the ship could have heard the small burst of sound deep in the bowels of the vessel where the engine room was located. If they had, they would have been scrambling like ants at a picnic in order to repair the small but effective damage done to the resting engine. So absorbed in the approach of the sleek helicopter were they that they also missed the second muffled pop that punched a small hole in one of the lowest of the ship's seams.

From his perch in the small heaving lifeboat, the man could tell exactly when their first inkling came that something was wrong. He smiled as the ship tilted slightly more than it should have in the Bay's choppy waters. The Captain turned away from the rail and his retreating passengers, tossing orders to his men, and then he turned a wicked eye back to the lifeboat. The man saluted him, the smile widening on his face. From somewhere aboard, a crew member shouted that the ship had sprung a leak.

The first mate scrambled to the bridge with the intent of turning the vessel to shore, but as he fired up the engine, the previously small damage ballooned into a loud explosion and black smoke roiled up from the stairwell that led to the ship's center.

The Captain clutched the rail and bellowed for his men to jump ship and head for shore. If the freezing water didn't kill them, they might find a way to civilization using the small row boat that was already making its way to land.

Amidst the backdrop of distant shouts the man felt the muffled scrape of the boat's contact with the gravel of the shore and he calmly stepped from the still bobbing craft. From the small cargo area of the helicopter the pilot pulled out a can of gasoline and offered it to his boss. He shook his head in refusal. Let the pilot do it.

He watched dispassionately as his pilot poured the can of liquid over the lifeboat, then he smiled again as tongues of yellow and red flame leapt from the wooden structure, consuming it in an instant conflagration. He cast a sly glance at the small figures splashing stiffly in the frigid waters. The fire loudly broadcast their fate to them in the heat waves and smoke that plunged skyward, shifting and gyrating with the increasing rotation of the chopper's blades. He stood a few moments longer, enjoying the life-giving heat, watching as it faded into weak embers. Then he nodded to his pilot and settled himself in a back seat, leaving the front passenger seat to his associate in crime. The sleek bird rose in the air, hovered for a moment, and then slowly lifted above the smouldering ruins to the clearer air.

The man continued to watch as the crew struggled and splashed their way toward shore. Few of them would make it through the arctic waters, and those who did would not likely survive in the harsh tundra. The ship sank quickly, its heavy diesel engine pulling it under the icy waves. Within minutes no sign of it remained other than a dark shadow beneath the churning surface of the Bay. One by one, the men of the small fishing vessel *The Swordfish* slipped beneath the waters as they, too, succumbed to the frigid darkness. He nodded to himself and reached forward to tap his pilot's shoulder. He'd seen enough. No witnesses. That's what he had decided. That's what he got. The chopper tilted and sped off toward the south, leaving the land as it had been. Empty. Stark. Barren. Incredible.

Yes. Nunavut was a place only for those who were gifted in the art of survival.

~~~Chapter One

IT COULD BE quite embarrassing being the only son of *Star Trek* enthusiasts. Especially when one's parents decided to name their son after its main star. But James Kirk Benedict had long ago resigned himself to the unusual handle. He had to grudgingly admit that it had even strengthened him somewhat. One couldn't go through twelve years of public schooling with a name like that and not find a little backbone. He did, however, manage to shorten it to James Benedict by the time he settled into university life, and now, as he pursued his career with the Federal Bureau of Investigations, few knew of the connection to the sci-fi show.

James plunked himself into a teak deck chair, closed his eyes and lifted his face to the distant sun, wishing that he had chosen a warmer place to sit. But he had privacy, and that was more important than gravitating to the warmer Lido and Promenade decks. Opening his eyes again, he scanned the horizon. The water in this chunk of the Pacific was the colour of slate and it heaved and churned around the cruise ship, bobbing it up and down like a giant cork. The Sky Deck had been a good choice for solitude, but he hoped the brisk wind wouldn't interfere with the last bit of his work before he could enjoy his fifteen-day cruise. With this amount of chop, few would venture so high without heaving the contents of their stomachs.

Slipping on a pair of sunglasses, he carefully opened his briefcase, prepared against any gust of wind eager to send his files into the drink. He pulled a manila envelope from the case's depths and quickly snapped the leather clasp closed again, setting it beneath his chair. *The Cassandra Carpenter File* was typed across the smooth yellow surface, and he withdrew the contents, feeling a knot twist into his gut as it did any time he worked on a child's case.

She was a real cutie, he thought as he looked at the glossy five-by-seven of a cherub-faced six-year-old girl with merry blue eyes and bobbing blond curls. Beneath it lay the photos taken at the scene of the crime. This child would never feel six again. Gone was the sanitized backdrop of the Grade One photo and in its place was a dark dungeon filled with human filth, rotting garbage and broken bits of metal and glass—and a small crumpled body. She lay on her side, facing the camera, vacant eyes staring into the lens. A paramedic hovered alongside, working to find a vein in the slim arm, captured forever on film in this single act of mercy. One after the other, the pictures stitched together scenes of a morbid and grim story. Battered and bruised victim. Clothes torn and cast aside. Tools of cruelty. Bits of newspapers and magazines with letters and words cut haphazardly from them.

James scanned the last photograph and dropped the bundle, still grasped carefully in a large hand, to his lap. He sighed as he lifted his eyes to the scene before him and wondered for the hundredth time why he didn't finish going over the file before he left for his long-awaited vacation. He probably should have left it on his tidy desk in San Diego, but he needed to know all the details for court. Thankfully, his partner Reese had agreed to tie up any loose ends while James was on vacation.

He thought back to the day they received the phone call from a concerned neighbour. It seemed that the perp was well-known for inviting kids into his house, something the neighbour didn't think was their business—until they recognized the kidnapped child on TV. James had come very close to using his service revolver that day. It was Reese's interference and that still small voice that had kept him from pulling the trigger on the man who had so cruelly tortured the little girl. He wasn't too sure, as he sat reflecting over the pictures, that he would have felt much remorse either. There were days that he still contemplated vengeance on behalf of the victims he came in contact with. And those were the days where his grandmother's Sunday school teachings would drift through his mind to remind him once more of her favourite Bible verse.

~*Revelation 7:17* ~

For the Lamb at the center of the throne will be their shepherd; he will lead them to springs of living water. And God will wipe away every tear from their eyes.

James gathered the pictures into a tidy bundle and evened the edges before clipping them together with a large paper clip and returning them to the envelope. Just because his grandmother was right didn't make it easy. Especially when he had to see the Cassandra Carpenters of the world and all they would have to endure to find some semblance of a normal life. The thought of the child's rehabilitation sidetracked James and he allowed himself the distraction. Cassandra had been sent for therapy with Dr. Julie Holding.

Julie. She always picked up where he left off in cases like this. He welcomed the intrusion as his mind took hold of the image of the Office for Victim Assistance psychologist. She was a woman that would take a lifetime to understand. The child and her family had just been moved into her capable hands. If she had her way, Jesus truly would, some day, wipe away this little girl's tears. But Julie had her work cut out for her.

Leaving the deck chair, James pulled himself up and wandered over to the glass lined edge of the cruise ship's top deck. He was a strange sight with his Hawaiian shirt tails peeking below the hem of his navy sweatshirt, baggy shorts flapping above socks and sandals and his briefcase clasped in a firm fist. Somehow he hadn't thought that the crisp San Diego winter weather would follow him out to sea. At any other time, he wouldn't be caught dead in socks and sandals, but the cool air gave him no choice. It was either that or wear his dress shoes and he wasn't sure that would be any better. He was just lucky that he had tossed the sweatshirt into his suitcase—just in case.

Allowing his gaze to stray across the horizon, he released a pent-up sigh. The sky had a leaden hue to it, blending into the choppy water that gave way to the sharply angled bow. He leaned an elbow on the oak railing and turned his mind back to the day before boarding the luxury cruise ship.

"I just can't go, James. Please don't ask me to." Julie's voice held a firm note and she raked her hand through her long dark hair. It was a sure indication that she was growing annoyed with a conversation that had repeated itself numerous times over the course of the last three months.

"How did you know I was going to ask you?" James experienced a mild sense of alarm and his fork froze on its way to his mouth. Julie knew far too often what was on his mind. He never understood the whole "women's intuition" thing and it sometimes made him a bit nervous that she could read him so well.

"Well, you were, weren't you?" A sudden smile twitched at the corners of her mouth as though she was on the edge of forgiving him for the slight trespass before he had even confessed to it.

He lowered his fork, abandoning the pasta dish. "Well—yes, I was—sort of. Actually, I was only going to express that it was a shame that we couldn't find some way to go on the same cruise ship without automatically leading people to believe that we'd be sharing a cabin. I wasn't going to ask you outright though. I already knew what your answer would be—again." He didn't like the sulk in his own voice.

"You and I both know that people will talk. It isn't assumed anymore that men and women who travel together aren't necessarily—together. Be that as it may, it's too late to make any changes anyway. I can't get the time off now even if I thought it was a good idea, and Cookie can't be left alone for two weeks."

James looked away, choosing not to comment on the cocker spaniel that had made it very plain that he wasn't welcome in Julie's life. He sighed and pushed the forkful of pasta into his mouth. He wasn't eager to disturb the evening's peace with memories of growls and teeth marks.

"Look, James," Julie's hand settled gently on his arm and he brought his eyes back to her face. "You know I'd love to go. I want to be with you but I also want to maintain my integrity before God. How can you and I show our co-workers that Christ means something to us if our actions don't reflect that? You know they'll talk, and as much as it doesn't matter to me on a human level, it most definitely does on a spiritual one."

Feeling the reprimand, James attempted a smile and turned the conversation to their busy week. "So what do you think of the new case? Do you think you can help Cassandra?"

Eyes as blue as the Pacific waters narrowed. While it was necessary for Julie to maintain a professional distance, it was a challenge she didn't always successfully rise to, especially when the victim was so young. "I'll do my best. I think I may ask for prayer support with the small group. No names. No details. I'll just tell them I have a child patient badly in need of emotional healing."

She twisted a strand of her curly brown hair around her finger. It was an endearing habit that told James her mind had plunged completely into the topic. Two weeks away from those all too familiar gestures wouldn't be easy.

The smile slipped from James' mouth and his eyes clouded. "I'm really going to miss you." Reaching up, he took hold of the hand and unwound the strand of hair, giving it a gentle tug.

Julie allowed her hand to slip into his and she shrugged. "I'll miss you too, but it *is* only two weeks. Soon enough, it'll be over and you'll be back, all rested and ready to dive back into your job of saving the world. I'll be here waiting. And Cookie too." She smiled impishly then, well aware of the animosity between the man she loved and the animal she loved.

James snorted and wiped his mouth. "Yes, I'm sure Cookie will be thrilled to see me again. I still have the marks from the last time she was overcome with love for me. I hope you won't be offended if I don't miss the dog?" He watched Julie's smile dim a bit and tried for a lighter tone. "Tell you what. When I get back, I'll buy a nice little juicy bone for her and maybe—just maybe—she won't be so concerned when I try to kiss you."

"Cookie's not here now." Her eyes deepened and James swallowed.

"No. No, she's not. But we *are* in a restaurant." He liked the direction this conversation was taking.

"Well, I'm finished if you are. And a nice walk would be just the thing to finish off the evening with my favourite guy." Julie rose and pushed her chair into the table. Without another word, she turned and headed for the cash register. James knew what was coming and scrambled to his feet, knowing that if he didn't get to the counter first, she would pay the bill. While he didn't have a problem with a woman picking up the tab, he very much had a problem with Julie paying when he had suggested the dinner out. "This is my treat." He pushed a bill onto the counter while she fumbled with her purse and grinned as she pinned him with a look and then snapped the clasp shut.

"Then, thank you for a lovely dinner. My treat next time. Deal?"

James nodded his answer and took her hand as they sauntered out into the cool evening. They chatted about insignificant things as the crisp breeze wrapped them in the scent of fresh ocean air. Papery leaves rustled in the darkened night, sighing as though relishing the romantic scene beneath. Wandering into a small park, James stopped her and turned Julie to face him. "I know you don't want to hear it, but I do still wish you were coming with me. Then I wouldn't have to say goodbye for two weeks."

"James, can't you just let it go?" She sounded tired. "Let's just enjoy the moment, ok?" Lifting her hands, she placed them on either side of his face and pulled him down to her. The kiss she had hinted of moments earlier lingered, filled with deep emotion, conveying her feelings more than words could. And then it was gone and they were left facing each other, the impish glint back in her eyes. "And Cookie wasn't here to interfere." She dropped her hands to his collar, straightening it out of habit. "Just enjoy your holiday and remember me on occasion. Like I said, I'll be here when you get back."

PUSHING A HAND against his unruly black hair, James allowed his mind to linger a bit longer on that kiss. He was seriously considering a more permanent commitment to Julie, obstinate cocker spaniel notwithstanding. But could they juggle their careers and still foster a relationship? And how would they approach the idea of a family of their own in such a tumultuous and emotionally draining environment? It wasn't the first time these questions had come to mind. It likely wouldn't be the last.

Gathering up his briefcase, he abandoned his post at the bow of the ship, hunched into the brisk wind and headed down the stairs that led to the elevator. He was badly in need of a warm room and a good cup of coffee. Shivering, he slipped into the marble-floored elevator and punched the button that would drop him to the promenade deck and then leaned back to watch the numbers announce each floor as it passed. A small chime rang and the doors shushed open to the foyer on deck four and he began the long trek to the rear of the ship where his stateroom waited.

With a swipe of his plastic key, James slipped into the tiny room that he would call home for the next two weeks. He removed the Carpenter file from the briefcase and carefully laid the papers in the cabin safe, punching in a personal code to secure the lock. He then deposited the empty briefcase into his open suitcase, which he then proceeded to close, lock and stuff under the bed. Pulling his sweater over his head, he returned to the hall and the staircase that would lead him up one deck to the coffee lounge. A staff member with a broad smile, heavy accent and name plate with *Jan* engraved on it greeted him warmly as he slid onto a tall stool at the coffee counter. "What is your pleasure, sir?"

James returned the smile. "A large black please." He waited patiently while the young man placed the steaming brew before him and he wrapped his cool hands around the mug and sipped slowly, grateful for the liquid warmth that ran the length of his esophagus. He was in the middle of his second cup of coffee when his satellite phone rang. Several patrons in the coffee bar looked his way, surprise and annoyance flickering over their faces. He had the sense to look guilty for having his phone turned on while on a cruise. The truth was he never really felt connected without it. Offering a timid smile, he flipped the instrument open and spoke softly into it. "Benedict here."

"You told me to call." Julie's warm tones filled his ear and his face lit up.

"So I did." Leaning on his elbow, he turned away from his fellow vacationers and his smile broadened. "What's up in your world today?"

"Well . . . you weren't joking when you said Cassandra Carpenter would be a real challenge, but I won't get into the details. Just pray for her, ok?"

He nodded. "I haven't stopped." Silence filled the receiver. "I could use some prayers myself. More and more, I'm wishing I'd put that guy out of his misery. Nobody deserves to live after doing something like that." He sighed, knowing what Julie would say.

"'Vengeance is mine,' says the Lord . . ." He could hear the concern in her voice.

"I know. That's why he put you in my life—so you could keep me on the right track. I miss you, you know."

"I miss you too. And I don't want to hear you say that I should have gone with you. A part of me is already regretting that decision."

James could hear the wistfulness in her tone and he sighed. "I know. I probably shouldn't have tempted you with the offer. It was purely innocent, but you're right—people talk even when there isn't anything to talk about. Someday. It'll happen the right way. I promise."

"If we can ever get our lives organized enough." The conversation had slipped into its familiar pattern: talking about the inevitability of marriage—*if* their schedules would work. "I'd better get back to work. Some of us don't get the luxury of sitting in the sun all day. I just needed to hear your voice again."

His smile broadened and he took on a bantering tone. "Well, those of us who do have the luxury haven't found the sun yet. I look a bit silly in sandals and socks. I don't know why I thought the temperature would rise the minute we got off shore. Oh well." He sighed his mock misery. "I'll just have to suffer through. I'll give you a call later so I can tuck you in for the night."

Julie snorted. "By the looks of the Carpenter case, I'm going to be busy trying to figure out a way to get the poor child to talk. I don't think bedtime will come too early for a few nights."

"Just don't overdo it. I don't want to come back all refreshed just to find you exhausted and burnt out. And I'm getting to the stage where our schedules are going to get rearranged permanently. This is the last cruise I'm going on without you. Deal?"

He could hear her smile again.

"Deal. You enjoy yourself and I'll talk to you tonight."

"I love you, Jules." It was a whisper.

"I love you too. Come home all safe and tanned, ok?"

He hit the end button and felt the smile slip from his face. So much for a relaxing holiday away. He missed her too much already.

Chapter Two

IN A CRAMPED office buried deep beneath the bowels of a concrete and steel monstrosity of a building, a man sat at his desk, a sullen expression fixed on his shadowed skin. He absently tapped a pencil on the chipped surface of his desk as his eyes wandered over the small case that had just arrived via courier. His father's medals. Newly mounted. Encased in wood and glass with a black velvet backdrop, they were all that remained of his father's service years in Vietnam. The Vietnam Civil Actions Unit Citation, the Vietnam Campaign Medal, the Gallantry Cross. All mementos of his father's call to duty. And his own personal loss. His mind drifted back to that time and he set aside the pencil and reverently stroked the beautiful casing.

His father had been a private for so long: since before his marriage and the birth of his only son. He had been a good soldier. But not an outstanding one. Vietnam changed all that—and him. His unit was one of the first waves of soldiers sent on March 8, 1965, to that mysteriously exotic corner of the world. To a place where he had to learn to be outstanding—or die.

August 18, 1965, brought with it Operation Starlite, and his father had written home about how proud he was to be in the first wave. What the boy's mother wasn't told were the details of his father's small stash of drugs carried into battle with him and how the man had felt the first addictive high of heroine just before his unit moved on the Viet Cong stronghold on the Van Tuong peninsula in the Quang Ngai Province. The drug's effects, combined with the adrenaline surge, lifted the boy's father out of the ranks of the average foot soldier into class of the elite, earning him his first medal and a promotion to Lance Corporal.

Over the course of the next five years, the boy's father shifted from battle to battle, fighting tenaciously, striving for more and more recognition—sinking deeper and deeper into heroine dependency. With each accomplished objective, he moved up the ladder of rank, finally attaining Sergeant. And then the day came that ended his ambition.

The bullet hit the soldier in the thick muscle of the thigh. It should have come out that day and healed beautifully. That was what the army doctors had said, anyway. In the letter home he had cursed the bullet for not taking his life. What good was he without a leg?

And so he was decommissioned. 1970. The boy was six and didn't know his father. The soldier was depressed, addicted, violently angry and showed signs of a strange illness that the army doctors couldn't explain. The boy watched helplessly as his father endured the agony of a disease that began with painful lesions behind the ears and under the arms. Soon cysts and pustules spread to the groin area and across gaunt cheeks. Hyperhidrosis followed, leaving the soldier perpetually soaked with sweat, and at this point the boy began to actively avoid him when the stench became too much to bear. And then blisters rose and covered the surface of the already tender skin and he couldn't stand to even look at him.

The soldier went to the army doctors time and again, badgering them for anything they could give him to kill the pain, scheming for ways to get a heroine fix. The boy watched as his father gave up trying to use a prosthetic limb and settled into a wheelchair with defeated inevitability. And then the leukocytosis moved into the wasting body, shooting the man's white blood cell count up to an unbelievable 29 x 109/L, elevating his lymphocyte count until the doctors could only use one phrase to describe the horror growing in him. Chronic terminal cancer.

On December 5, 1974, a year before the end of the Vietnam War, this war hero, heroine addict and one-legged father of a ten-year-old boy died—a shadow of his former self. The boy stood in the wind that whipped through the snow covered cemetery, mourning for the sore-infested skeleton and the loss of the man he had never really known. His mother stood at his side, her tears long ago dried up.

The buzzing of a telephone brought that young boy back to the present. Back into the body of a forty-one-year-old man. He set the medals aside and forced his mind and emotions back into the dark cubicle as he picked up the phone. "Yes, Doris?"

The nasal voice came back at him in bored tones. "You have a call, sir. Would you like me to patch it through or should I take a message?"

He weighed both options, quickly deciding that he was far too emotional right now to make rational decisions. "Take a message, Doris. If it's something that you think we shouldn't pass up, give Harry a call with it. Give me a half hour or so. Ok?" Doris hesitated. She was likely shocked that he had rejected the call. That wasn't like him at all. He never passed up a business opportunity.

He pressed the button to terminate the connection and allowed his mind to finish its train of thought. It wasn't until years later that he had discovered the reasons behind his father's death. The mysterious cancer was caused by dioxin poisoning. His father had received massive doses of the stuff while fighting a war that wasn't his country's to fight. Polychlorinated Dibenzo Dioxin. Better known as Agent Orange. Or another of the rainbow chemicals used to defoliate the jungles of Vietnam.

Nor did he find out until the '90's that the U.S. military command in Vietnam, while insisting it was safe, sprayed it full strength up to twenty-five times the manufacturer's suggested rate. By 1966 they had dumped just over two million gallons across that beleaguered country's landscape. But they knew. They all knew. The makers of the wicked concoctions. The government officials. The Air Force scientists. Even the army doctors treating his father knew. Their precious "Project Pink Rose" was far more important than the health of their own soldiers.

And so one small boy watched his father die a horrible death. Watched his mother struggle with the overwhelming medical bills and the trauma that came from being one man's punching bag. Stood at her graveside too, after she succeeded with one of her many desperate suicide attempts.

And while uncaring leaders moved on with their lives, distancing themselves from the horrors they had created, he entered his own private world of terror.

Shuffled off to foster home after foster home, with only his father's medals as a token remembrance stuffed carefully in a battered shoebox, the boy grew into manhood.

Tipping back in his creaking office chair, he thought about where he had come from and where he'd ended up. What did he really have? His parents were gone. He had no siblings, no real family to share his life. He had been left with a handful of ribbons and engraved steel. And a deep, slowly awakening anger.

~Chapter Three

THE GENERAL SETTLED his plump pink carcass into a teak deck chair parked beneath the retractable awning that stretched high above the salt water pool on the Lido deck. A drink waited by his elbow for his consumption and he basked in the warmth of the great dome's protective glass shield. He had just visited one of the ship's shops to buy a small bauble for his wife. It was amazing luck that they had won the cruise tickets mere weeks before their anniversary. Of course, he wouldn't tell her that. What did it hurt to let her think that he had planned the whole thing? The small card accompanying the complimentary bottle of wine that had been left in their room was quickly snatched into his meaty hand and dropped in a garbage basket. And they had shared a toast to their fifty years together. He would have done something to commemorate the accomplishment, but he wasn't a creative man. Forty years in the military had seen to that. A cruise would have never come to mind.

He watched his wife briefly as she splashed in the pool, her portly girth comparable to his own, and then his eyes flickered over to the younger, slimmer women, scantily clad in bikinis and ready for him to devour through the dark lenses of his sunglasses. *If they only knew what they do to men when they wear those things*, he mused as he reached for and drained the last of his rye and coke. His stomach rumbled violently with a suddenness that surprised and embarrassed him, and he flicked a glance around to see if his digestive murmurings had been overheard. All the other nearby passengers were either engrossed in books, sleeping or, like him, ogling the unsuspecting beauties in their swimwear. He smiled briefly and returned to his pastime.

Across the deck, a small waiter of Indo-Asian origins watched the General keenly while he gathered some of the guests' dirty dishes and glasses from off the patio tables. He allowed himself a small smile, noting with satisfaction that the General's skin tone had paled somewhat underneath the carefully groomed tan. It would only be a few hours and the vengeance would begin.

Tip carried his loaded tray around the broad deck of the pool with the intention of returning to the kitchen. He made certain his path crossed behind the General's over-burdened chair so he could collect the empty glasses. It wouldn't do to have someone discover the drink. He approached the man, marvelling at how quickly this particular cocktail was taking affect. Nam had said it would be fast and lethal. He wasn't joking. "Sir, can I get you another drink?" He hated the cheesy, ingratiating voice he was forced to adopt around the spoiled guests. It made him sound so weak and Tip was certainly not a weak man. Quiet?

Yes. Solitary? Most definitely. But never weak. Childhood had seen to that.

The General grunted his refusal and began to grip his abdomen. Tip carefully retrieved the glass and left him to his suffering. Keeping the tray carefully balanced, he headed toward the bar where he could unload it, at the same time casually lowering the single contaminated glass into his pants pocket. Quickly, he slipped into the small kitchen behind the bar and emptied the heavy tray and then, before anyone could engage him in a new task or conversation, he stalked back out, tray in hand. Discreetly, he grabbed an open can of cola and dumped it down the opposite side of his pants and jacket and then let out a curse loud enough to be heard by a fellow waiter who had just slipped in behind the bar.

"What's up?" the co-worker said.

"I just spilled a drink down my jacket. Can you cover for me while I go change? Quickly?"

His associate grinned and nodded. "Sure, klutz. Go ahead. I'll cover but don't take long."

No one, except for the other crew member, noticed him leave the pool area and disappear down the staff staircase to the lower depths of the ship. Nor did they see him pitch the glass overboard from the main aft deck. Only one other person—a cabin steward—saw him cut through the deep confines of the ship's bowels with the intention of changing his soiled clothing. That wasn't unusual. He wasn't the first to spill food on himself and he wouldn't be the last.

Tip hurried. He didn't want to miss the show. The taste of sweet revenge was already pumping adrenaline through his veins. His small cabin, shared with a fellow waiter, was tidy to the point that it looked uninhabited. He kept it that way out of obsession. This was the one part of his world over which he had some semblance of control. He carefully rifled through his clean laundry, drawing out another change of clothing. Quickly, he slipped out of the soiled uniform and redressed, tossing the messy garments into a small basket that would later be taken to the laundry chute. And then he almost ran to the upper deck, eager to see how far his handiwork had progressed.

The General was wheezing by the time Tip returned to his post and the small waiter noted with concealed pleasure that the portly man's lips were beginning to turn blue. Another deck hand had noticed the older man's distress and called for medical help. Already, a small crowd had begun to gather. Tip remained in the background, watching it all, feeling nothing except the pain that came from remembering his own suffering as he watched his parents' bodies rot away, left as unattended corpses in a village wiped clean by the greed of their enemies. Two sturdy medical officers gently hoisted the General's bulk onto a stretcher and manoeuvred him off the deck, his dripping wife fussing alongside. Tip knew where to find the man when he needed to do so and he hungered for his reaction to what he would tell him.

~~~Chapter Four

H E HADN'T HEARD from Sandy in just over a year. They had graduated university together. Alexander Harridan. Shy business type. Self-made billionaire. Nice guy. James pondered the man's success as he wandered through to the dining room dressed in his formal wear. The owner of the cruise line had pulled out all the stops when he designed and decorated the ship and James' loyalty to his friend had made the decision to choose *The Cormorant* an easy one. Sandy likely wouldn't even know that James was aboard one of his ships. He'd have to give him a call after the vacation was over and let him know what he thought.

Strolling down the plush carpet, he absorbed the smell of cigarette smoke from the noisy casino as it mingled with the rich fragrance of buttered popcorn from the movie theatre. A hint of expensive perfume added to the strange buffet of scents, and he sneezed. Picking up the pace, he wandered past jewellery stores, bars and lounges until he had covered the entire Upper Promenade Deck. *Yep, Sandy has certainly gone all out.*

"It's just horrible! The poor man looked like he was about to explode and his skin was the awfullest green I've ever seen!"

The emphatic conversation drifted back to James from two little old ladies trussed up in their finest and dripping with jewellery. He honed in on the dialogue out of force of habit. FBI training was pretty thorough.

"I heard that he died shortly after! His wife is just a mess. She says he was all covered with boils. She didn't even get to say goodbye. I've asked a few of the staff members, but they just keep saying that they're looking into it. If I didn't know better, I'd swear they're trying to keep something secret." The blue-haired biddy tisked sadly and bustled toward the Diamond Dining Room. "I hope it's nothing contagious. I just had a skin treatment done and I'd hate to have it ruined with sores."

"Oh my! I never thought of that!"

James worked to keep the snort from escaping his mouth as he mentally shook his head. The stories that traveled around a cruise ship were beyond belief. It was more likely that the old boy had had a heart attack or a bad case of the flu. He entered the roomy dining hall and settled himself at his assigned table set for eight, smiling to his table mates. Reese would have a laughing fit if he could see him all spiffed up in tux and tie. It wasn't exactly his regular work attire. And what would Julie think? He smiled as he thought about her reaction and pulled at the tight collar.

A fifty-something couple settled next to him and he smiled a greeting. The woman was tall and lean and showed very little of her accumulated years. Her husband pulled out the chair beside James and helped her settle comfortably before parking himself on her other side. Two other couples were there before James arrived and the final place at the table was reserved for a member of the officer crew—an engineer. It was the cruise line's way of making certain no one felt left out. As the introductions were made, James immediately veered away from discussions of his career out of force of habit. Turning to the woman beside him, he immediately launched into conversation. "And you're a retired army nurse? Well, it's very nice to meet you, Mrs. Harris."

"Please call me Mary Anne. And this is my husband, Michael." Mary Anne's eyes crinkled with pleasure and she offered a hand.

Reaching out, James grasped his new acquaintance's hand in a firm handshake.

HE WAS ON the golf course when the call came in. Alone. He did most things alone. He had never been able to get past the idea that people more interested in what he had than in who he was. He handed his golf club to the caddy and flipped open the cell phone. Only one person would be calling this number. "It went well?"

The voice bearing a slight Asian accent answered in a brief quiet sentence. "As you said it would."

He walked away from the caddy, gesturing to the younger man to stay with the cart and clubs. "Did you tell him before he died?"

"Yes." Silence followed.

He switched the phone to his other ear and tossed a glance at the caddy leaning against the cart—the man was wise enough to look the other way. "I suppose this is the beginning, then. When things quiet down, move on to the next target. But don't take too long. You've only got fifteen days to cover them all." He flipped the phone shut, walked back to the cart and selected a putter. The shot was subtle and gentle and the ball whispered smoothly across the groomed green to plop with finality into the cup.

His day was going extraordinarily well so far.

SHE HAD BEEN a nurse during the war. A quiet woman. Gentle and caring. Or so many of the soldiers had thought. But she had taken one look at the young man lying on the pallet, his leg swollen with the penetration of a well-aimed bullet, and decided quickly. Too quickly. Had she shown an extra measure of compassion and looked closer, she would have seen that the leg was already beginning to fester. But there were others who drew her attention so she moved on. The soldier was forgotten until long after the gangrene set it. And then it was too late. So instead of a limp and a normal existence, he was condemned to life in a wheelchair. And despair. Her name was on the list. Mary Anne Harris. Wife. Mother. Grandmother. And her offspring would soon know what it meant to lose someone they loved.

MARY ANNE LOOKED lovely in her formal evening gown. She was a remarkably fit woman for being in her sixties and was grateful for her healthy physique. Unable to see her own beauty, she marvelled at the devotion of her husband of thirty-six years and was willing to do just about anything she could to hang on to him for as many years as she had left.

They enjoyed their table mates in the formal dining hall, laughing and sharing small tidbits of their lives with the six other people. She didn't often eat desert, but it was their first formal dinner and she felt it safe to indulge a little. Chocolate had always been her one weakness and she eyed the lavish deserts eagerly.

The friendly young waiter smiled broadly and held the desert tray before the guests, explaining each dish with affection, as though every one of them was his own favourite creation. Mary Anne nodded her agreement at his recommendation of the chocolate truffle. What would it hurt?

The desserts arrived with a flourish, and each of the guests savoured the rich confections. Mary Anne hadn't even finished her truffle when a wave of nausea hit her. Slowly, she pushed her plate away and pressed her hand against her stomach, hoping it would pass. She wasn't prone to sea sickness, but there was always a first for everything. Reaching for her water glass, she took a long pull on the drink, hoping it would help. It didn't.

"Are you alright, dear?" Patricia was the wife of a retired doctor and had a motherly way about her. At present, she wore a concerned frown and her eyes perused Mary Anne with a professionalism that led one to think she, too, had been a doctor. "Alfred, she looks quite pale all of a sudden, don't you think?"

Her husband had been deep in conversation with the men of the table and excused himself to throw a brief glance at the woman. And then he looked closer, alarmed at what he saw. Her face was beaded with sweat and her lips were turning blue. Eyes that had previously been bright with intelligence were suddenly glazed and dull. "Mary Anne, can you hear me? Are you alright?" He reached forward then and lifted a limp arm, automatically feeling for her pulse. And as his table mate slowly toppled against her husband's shoulder, the doctor was up and reaching for her carotid artery to find a clearer heart rate.

Quietly, discreetly, Mary Anne and her husband were ushered from the dining hall and whisked away to the medical quarters. And while the attention was on the departing group, a dish of half-eaten truffle was wrapped in a serviette and slipped away to be permanently discarded.

Within a few hours, Mary Anne died. A look of horror was fixed upon her blotched and bloated face and she was laid to rest in cold storage beside the body of the predeceased General. Her husband was ushered to his cabin, where he poured out his grief in quarantined quarters. And a ship to shore call was made from the medical offices of *The Cormorant*.

Chapter Five

JAMES HIT THE end button on his cell phone, snapped the unit shut and ran a distracted hand through his dark hair. "I've contacted my superior. You couldn't ask for anyone better. Special Agent in Charge Steve St. Kitts. He'll know the best way to handle all of this."

"Thank you so much for your assistance, Special Agent Benedict." The ship Commander's voice was soft and measured, as though he weathered half a dozen emergency situations on a daily basis. "I've already informed the cruise line owner of the situation. Mr. Harridon was quite pleased to hear you were on board. He has quite a bit of faith in your skills."

James drew a tight smile and nodded in acknowledgement of the compliment. "University loyalty, no doubt. I'd like to make some more phone calls, if you don't mind, Captain Van den Breck. Steve has suggested that I contact the head of the Center for Disease Control. He'd do it, but he pointed out that I'd have to call to describe the symptoms anyway."

"By all means. In the meantime, I have a ship to run. Thank you for making yourself available, Mr. Benedict." The tall Dutchman bowed slightly, threw a measured look around the medical facility's office and stalked from the room, leaving James to place his next call. He tried to shut out, as he punched in a phone number he was all too familiar with, the vision of Mary Anne Harris' lovely face swollen and covered in pustules.

"Center for Disease Control. How may I help you?"

"This is Special Agent James Benedict. Could I please speak to Dr. Perry O'Connell? It's an emergency." The silver-haired doctor was someone James had relied on heavily in the past and he knew the older man's analytical mind would assess what little they knew, ultimately ending up with the best course of action. To James, the whole thing was shaping up to a potentially unknown virus and the only good thing about it was the ship's isolation. If it was contagious, it was, at least, confined.

"This is Dr. O'Connell speaking." The voice was firm and clipped in spite of the echo that accompanied it.

"This is Special Agent James Benedict, Dr. O'Connell. From the San Diego Bureau. I have a situation on my hands and I need your direction."

"Yes, James. I thought you were on vacation. You didn't change your mind, now, did you? It's not good to put your work ahead of everything else."

James smiled at the paternal tone. "No, Dr. O'Connell. I took my vacation but it seems that work likes to tag along. I've got two bodies on board here. Male and female. Not related. They've both died of the same symptoms and you're not going to like what you hear."

"Go on." The voice shifted and became all business.

"Perry, these people died fast and horribly. They were covered with sores, soaked in sweat and died within hours of symptom onset. The woman was my table mate. She was healthy one minute and then passed out the next. I actually watched the sores break open on her face and arms. I've never seen anything like it before."

"Are the spouses sick?"

James shook his head. "No, that's the strange thing. None of the spouses are showing any signs, but then, the victims didn't either. And then, they did. And then, they were dead." He sighed and ran his hand through his hair again. If he kept it up, he wouldn't have much hair left.

"James, listen carefully. This could be a viral outbreak, which I assume you already guessed or you wouldn't have called me. You need to get the spouses to a place where you can keep an eye on them but they're away from the rest of the passengers and crew. They're not going to like the isolation, but that's just the way it needs to be until we find out if they're in some sort of incubation period. The victims may have contracted a virus—if, indeed, it is one—and the spouses are next in line. Thank God this is happening on a ship. At least it can't spread beyond the ship."

"I thought of that, although I'm not exactly thrilled to be part of it all myself."

James thought of Julie then and how glad he suddenly was that she hadn't joined him. "We've quarantined the spouses to their cabins for now. I'll make certain that someone phones them regularly to make certain they are alright. Food trays and supplies are left outside their doors."

"Is there any way you can get tissue samples to me? I'm going to need all major organs, blood, hair, anything you can think of. I'm sure the medical officer on board ship will have all the necessary equipment to accommodate. Those cruise ship medical centers are pretty impressive."

"Not a problem. I'll figure something out. Is there anything else I need to know?"

"Just be careful, James. And get those samples to me ASAP. If it moves as fast as you say, this could become an epidemic, and I will need to know how to deal with that. Let me know what you come up with."

James signed off and dropped the phone into its cradle.

"So what's the plan?" The Chief Medical Officer was a middle aged Russian woman with short-cropped greying brown hair. The nameplate pinned to her neatly pressed uniform read *Yanina Petruscov*. She was the kind of doctor James didn't think patients argued with often.

"He wants tissue samples of every kind and I need to find a way to get them to him without spreading this if it's a communicable disease." He scratched the short bristles of his newly growing beard and frowned.

"Why don't you just set them adrift in one of the lifeboats?"

James shook his head. "No. We may need the boats at some point." He flicked a half-amused glance at her. "I know. One disaster at a time. No. We need something disposable. What about life jackets?"

Yanina nodded. "I could check with the Security Officer. Mick would know if that's feasible. I'm sure we have plenty of extra life jackets." She snatched up the ship phone and punched in the code that would link her directly to the security office. "Is Security Officer Lang there, please? Yes. Mick? Do we have a surplus of life jackets? I thought so. Can we dispose of, say, ten without any trouble? I'll explain later. Could you have someone bring them to me at the Medical Center? You will? Fine, a Special Agent from the FBI will be here to receive them. He can explain the situation. Yes, it does have to do with the deaths, but I don't think a ship communications system is a good way for you to receive this information." Her voice had become clipped and James could see she was clearly annoyed. "I'll see you shortly, then." She hung up the phone and offered a ghost of a smile. "Security Officer Lang will be here quicker than you expect."

James nodded and watched her head to the examination room and the storage rooms beyond where the two bodies lay in narrow refrigerated lockers. She would likely have the samples ready by the time the security officer arrived too. Yanina was the kind of woman who continually redefined the meaning of the word efficient.

Chapter Six

"SYLVIA, GET ME as much information as you can on one General Karl MacCollum and a Mrs. Mary Anne Harris. I want everything you can possibly find—birth weight, when they first walked, paper route, school records, the last time they hiccupped—everything. And as quickly as you can."

"Yes, sir." The line went dead before Special Agent in Charge Steve St. Kitts could say any more. Without hesitation, he punched in the series of digits that would lead him to James Benedict's satellite cell phone. Picking up a pencil, he began to doodle absently along the edges of the thick pad of paper filled with neatly scrawled notes.

"Benedict here." The voice sounded as clear as if James were in the room.

"Give me everything you've got so far, James."

"Can I call you back, sir? I'm not in a secure area. Give me five minutes."

The line went dead and Steve dropped the phone into its cradle and stared at it off and on as he rifled through the various stacks of papers piled neatly on his desk. When the ring finally came, he snatched up the instrument before it finished its first tone. "Yes?"

"Ok, sir, this is what I've got. You already know that two are dead and I've given you all the symptoms that I know. Dr. Petruscov has all the tissue samples ready for Dr. O'Connell and we've got a raft rigged out of life jackets so we can set the case adrift. You're going to have to find a way to pick up the samples, but we'll set off the life jackets' GPS beacons just in case the currents take them too far before you get here.

"Steve, Dr. Petruscov is worried—and she doesn't strike me as the worrying kind."

Steve leaned forward intently. "What's she worried about?" His pencil tapping stilled.

James' voice cut through the airwaves. The tension could easily be heard. "She said the internal organs were a mess. She's never seen anything like it. None of it made sense to her and when I asked her to explain it further she clammed up. She just told me to wait for Dr. O'Connell's report. She didn't want to say in case it interfered with our findings. Said she'd tell me after we got Perry's report. Steve, we need to get this stuff to Perry right away."

"I'll send a chopper and a retrieval team ASAP, James. I'll give them your cell so they can contact you directly. That way they can be there before you launch the samples. I'm sorry it's wrecked your holiday, James, but I've got to say that I'm glad you're on board. I hope it isn't what we're all thinking it is." Steve leaned back into his chair then and tossed a worried look out the wall of windows.

"If it isn't, then we'll be looking for something just as bad."

"Oh?"

"If it isn't a virus, then it has to be poison. That means we may have a killer on our hands."

"YOU'RE LATE." Julie didn't accuse. She stated facts. It probably came from spending ten hours each day analyzing people's actions, thoughts and emotions. And James could hear the smile behind the tone.

"It's been a busy day." Even to himself, James' voice sounded tired.

"I've heard. Were you going to tell me that you are sitting on a floating incubator for a deadly virus, or is this one of those things that you can't share?"

It could have come off sounding resentful but Julie wasn't really the resentful type. There was, however, a shift in the inflection. James sensed her worry. "I didn't want to jump the gun. How'd you find out? I haven't even gotten the tissue samples to Perry yet."

Julie chuckled into the receiver. "You've forgotten so soon who your partner is? Reese has been in and out of here all day pumping me for information. He's worried about you too, you know, and Steve St. Kitts is pretty tight lipped so Reese probably figured I'd be the next best available source. Imagine his surprise when I didn't know a thing about it." She chuckled in an effort to rid her voice of its tight sound. "Don't worry. I haven't shared with anyone else a thing he's said. I'm bureau-trained too, remember.

But if Reese wants information, he's going to have to get it from you or Steve."

James sighed heavily. "It doesn't matter where I go; I seem to bring my work with me. Not that I planned it that way. This really isn't the kind of job that's conducive to a healthy relationship either. How do you put up with it—and with me?"

"I knew the risks when I let you charm me, Mr. Benedict."

Her gentle voice drifted along the invisible pathway that led to his cell phone and he soaked in the sound. "I assumed Steve would keep it on a need-to-know basis anyway. I'll have to call Reese and bring him up to date with everything once I get the okay from Steve. I've thought about it a couple times today, but I've been running crazy and haven't had the chance."

"Anything you can share?" Julie sounded interested but not pushy.

"Probably not, at this point. But you'll be on my list as the information comes in. How's your work going with Cassandra?" Silence filled the airwaves for a few moments and James hoped he hadn't offended Julie with the small brush off. Sometimes he really hated his job. He heard her answering sigh, and when she finally spoke, Julie's voice had dropped into deeper, clinical tones. Julie only did that when her job was painful for her.

"She's suffering a lot. But kids are pretty resilient. I've got her drawing pictures to help get the trauma out in the open. I'm praying that God will perform a real miracle here. No child should have to suffer like this." Her voice lifted again. "But beyond that, I can't really say a whole lot."

James chuckled and closed his eyes, pulling her image into the forefront of his mind. "So I guess we're going to have to tiptoe around some subjects for the next little while until it's safe to discuss them. I guess that leaves us with politics and religion to talk about."

"And hobbies and sports," she added.

James laughed then. "The last time we talked about hobbies and sports, you gave me a rough time."

"I just never heard of a man who liked to knit sweaters before. It took me by surprise. And if *I* remember correctly, you weren't so gentle about my stamp collecting. And that *is* a hobby done quite as often by women as men—unlike knitting."

James recalled the night of their first date when they had shared some of their interests in the dark Italian restaurant in 'Little Italy'. So what if he knitted sweaters? It was relaxing and he told her that. He could still see the saucy grin plastered across her face as she twisted a strand of her long dark hair around her finger. He had so badly wanted to wrap her in his arms and thoroughly kiss that grinning mouth. Instead, he stuffed a forkful of pasta into his mouth and when a stray noodle flipped up and spattered tomato sauce across his cheek, Julie laughed outright and wiped it away with her serviette. Someday soon, he was going to marry that woman.

The laughter of their reminiscence died away and silence held them for a few moments longer.

"I miss you, you know." Julie sounded wistful.

"I miss you too. I'm really beginning to wish that I had just stayed home."

"Hmm. A nice thought, but you really wouldn't have gotten the rest you need."

"And I'm getting it now?" James leaned out onto the railing that overlooked the churning waters in the ship's wake. His eyes squinted against winter's late afternoon sun as he looked toward San Diego's distant shores. "Sorry— that was a bit sharp. Julie, you and I are going to have a serious heart to heart when I get home after this. I'm pretty tired of spending my vacations without you."

"You only have to ask the question, James. You know that."

It was a whisper and James closed his eyes again. "Pray for me, Jules. Pray for us all. We're going to need it before this cruise is over."

"I already am. You didn't think I'd let you go off alone without my prayers behind you, now, did you?" The smile was back in her voice.

"I love you, Jules. Don't ever forget that."

"I love you too."

SPECIAL AGENT in Charge Steve St. Kitts paced his office with the nervous energy he was known for throughout the San Diego Bureau. Running manicured hands over his grey-ing coarse tightly-curled hair, he used his excess movement to focus the energy into thought. He had listened intently to all that Sylvia had reported, hoping that it was simply a series of coincidences and yet knowing that there were no such thing as coincidences in his line of work. "So they were both assigned to Vietnam during '65 to '70?"

The aging secretary nodded and dropped her eyes back to the hasty but detailed notes she had compiled. "Yes, sir. General Karl McCollum was one of the key officers involved in organizing the deployment of special operational troops in Nam over the course of that time and Mary Anne Harris was a nurse in one of the medical field units. That's the only connection we can find so far, other than the cruise ship. Maybe they contracted this disease, or whatever it is, in a restaurant they both shared within the past week. I'm still looking into every stop they've made in the last fourteen days."

Steve ceased his pacing and clamped his busy hands into surrender behind his back while he threw his gaze out the window and across the skyline of the city he had overseen for nearly twenty years. "Are all the arrangements made for the pickup? If this is a contagious disease, we don't need it coming inland, so I want it done right." Cold fingers of fear nudged at the base of Steve's spine as he contemplated the nightmare that could come about if the samples weren't handled properly. And then he clamped down his own concerns and focused on the details as Sylvia fired them off one by one in her smoke-roughened voice.

"I've contacted the ship and directed them to seal the samples once they've taken them. I told them to find a briefcase and sterilize the outside after the samples are packed. That way the disease can't transfer from the container to the boys handling it. They already had the idea to set them adrift from the ship when we're ready to pick them up. They've got plenty of life jackets so they're jerry-rigging something. When it's ready they'll set the beacon lights on the vests flashing and toss it overboard. I've talked to the chopper pilot and he plans on being there before it's launched. Says he's made all the arrangements with Special Agent Benedict."

The Special Agent in Charge continued his perusal of the city, offering a brief nod as his only response. When he continued to study the skyline, saying nothing more, Sylvia rose and headed for the door, knowing the meeting was at an end.

"Hold on a second, Sylvia. Have you done any research on Alexander Harridan? I know he was a colleague of James's, but how well do we really know him? It is his ship, after all. Maybe we should track down his records—just in case we need them."

Sylvia clicked her pen and scrawled a few notes in her chicken-scratch handwriting. "I can compile a file on him if you'd like. Is there anything else, sir?"

The man blew out an explosive sigh and turned to face his secretary. "No, that'll be all. And thanks Sylvia. Oh— could you send Reese Thomson in? I have a job for him. Maybe it'll keep him from pestering around for information."

He smiled a tight smile as the surly woman grunted and pulled the door closed behind her. Ignoring her brusque manner, Steve poured himself a cup of hours-old, varnish-thick coffee, lowered his lanky frame into the padded chair at his desk and turned his mind to the two files resting on the smooth surface. Moments later a brief knock interrupted his concentration and he slapped the covers closed and called out a clipped, "Come in!"

"You called for me, boss?" A toothy greying blond fifty-something man peeked his face around the solid wood door.

Steve frowned at the casual title—one he wasn't particularly fond of. "Yes, Reese. Come sit down. I have a job for you. Sylvia has just handed me these files and I don't really have time to dissect them properly. I want you to go through them and find any common ground between the two. They're the victims from the cruise ship." Steve watched Reese's brown eyes light up with interest and he fought back the knowing grin. "Yes, I suppose you are interested in James' cruise incident. Well, you're about to find out the correct way. That's all." Steve stood and handed the two files to the stocky agent. "And Reese? If you want to know something, ask me, not everyone else in the Bureau. Your curiosity could get people into trouble."

"Yes, sir." Reese tipped his head once, took the paperwork and let himself out.

Steve understood a partner's concern, but Reese needed to follow protocol. Hopefully, the gentle reprimand would remind him of that.

Chapter Seven

THE SHIP WAS silent, for the most part. Only the creaking of joints and fittings punctuated the stillness as the great lady moved within the embrace of the calm ocean. The quiet whispers of late staff footsteps were muted by the carpeting in the long halls as the cabin stewards and bar staff completed their final cleanup before they, too, settled down to sleep. The beast moved on, unconcerned with one small member of its population as he slipped from shadow to shadow, ever closer to the medical center nestled deep in *The Cormorant*'s forward hull.

The crew member wasn't supposed to be in the medical center unless it was absolutely necessary. There were emergency supplies provided in the stations where the Filipino and Indonesian crew were housed, but Tip wasn't there because of personal illness. His hand groped in the pocket of his waiter's pants, searching for the key he had lifted from the medical officer, and he peered down the halls cautiously. It wouldn't do to get caught.

Once more he found himself thinking about the ease with which he had managed to get aboard ship. One look at the Asian eyes and black hair and it was assumed he was just one more Indonesian looking for work. He slipped into the darkened office, mentally disgusted that people never really stopped to look beyond the basics. All the same, he was grateful for their ignorance. It had allowed him to fit into the Indonesian crew just that much more easily. That just showed how little people really paid attention. There was a vast difference between his kind and the Indonesian people, but no one cared to look that closely, and since he had lived in Jakarta long enough and spoke enough languages to make him an asset, he had been welcomed onto the staff with open arms and very few questions.

Shrugging against the incompetence, he shut and relocked the door behind him and then tiptoed to the refrigeration unit that held the tissue samples drawn from the two corpses. He couldn't have the samples analyzed until all those on the list were dead. By then, he wouldn't care if they knew what it was or where he had gotten it.

Pulling the case from the refrigeration unit, he slipped it onto a nearby table. A final glance toward the door told him that he was safe and he pulled a filtered breather from his pocket and slipped it over his nose and mouth. It was only a cheap felt one from the hardware store he had visited on shore, but hopefully it would be enough. He flipped the latch on the sealed carrying case, waving at the small puff of super-cooled vapour. And then he drew a small glass vial from a case he had brought with him.

Popping open each sample vial, he added a few drops of the pale liquid and swished it around to thoroughly saturate the contents. Each was resealed and returned to its place with great care, and then Tip slipped his case and the breather back into his pockets and left the medical center, intentionally dropping the medical officer's stolen keys onto the floor a few feet down the hallway. He smiled with relief, removed and pocketed his latex gloves, and after one last brief glance, slipped away to his own small cabin below.

EARLY IN THE morning, as the sunlight danced on the Pacific waters, tossing cascades of diamond-bright prisms through the air, a McDonnell Douglas 530 helicopter—known as the "Little Bird"—hovered low over a small florescent orange bundle that bobbed and wobbled in the chop created by the rapidly spinning rotor blades. A man dangled precariously from a rope that swayed above the small target in a manoeuvre that allowed the retrieval of the necessary tissue samples from the nearby cruise ship while also offering a chance for agents-in-training to practice an FBI "fast rope" exercise. Why not kill two birds with one stone?

Like a spider on a very large web, the man slipped quickly and smoothly down the rope's length to snatch the drifting parcel from the water and clip it to his nylon harness. And then, with practiced speed and efficiency, he scooted back up the rope into the waiting arms of his associates and the warmth of the chopper's interior. They were warned that the parcel wasn't to be opened and must be retrieved ASAP. With the pickup finished, the "Little Bird" swung around and headed back to its concrete nest on the shore.

A small party of spectators watched the proceedings solemnly, hoping that, very soon, the secured bundle would offer up answers to the serious problem they faced on their small, floating world. Commander Van den Breck finally sighed and turned back to the task at hand, hoping the answers would come before another passenger fell victim to the cruel ailment.

⁓Chapter Eight

"Why don't you just shut your trap, woman?" he hissed under his breath at the small lady who tittered nervously at his side. "You're making me mess up my shots."

Victor was one of those men who presented himself as a loudly boisterous and jovial man. But his wife knew differently. Annie stood there, her tight smile pasted to her face as she watched her husband swing at the small plastic golf ball.

They were at the edge of the Lido deck pool, caught in an intense round of golf Olympics, and Victor, fiercely competitive as some salesmen are prone to being, had just flubbed his second putt. If the truth be known, on a windy day such as this it would have taken a miracle to sink the lightweight ball into the life ring floating at the pool's center. But Victor didn't like defeat, and if he couldn't acknowledge its source, he would find one. Annie usually fit the bill.

She held her breath, her frightened eyes glued to the ball as, for the third time the putter connected and pushed it into the air. She prayed that, by some miracle, the wind would shift and carry the stupid ball to the sought-after goal. Plop. It landed a good foot short in the rippling and rocking water and she felt her heart race. Victor would admit defeat with a good-hearted wave, pat his competitors on the shoulders and find an excuse to beg off. Once the doors of their cabin closed, he would release his true feelings and Annie would find the right tone of makeup to hide the bruises.

Looking at her husband, she eyed him apprehensively, watching him enact the very scene she had just conjured in her mind. And then she looked closer. Victor was sweating profusely—something he seldom did. An athletic man, he would never hesitate to remove his shirt if he thought un-sightly sweat stains might appear. And he enjoyed showing those around him that he had a good physique for a man of sixty-three. But oddly, he had kept his shirt on, allowing it to soak with his body's moisture.

His stomach growled suddenly and he laughed a forced chuckle, commenting that it was time to feed the beast within. The others laughed in response and shook hands, enjoying the brief camaraderie before going their separate ways. Annie tensed as her eyes connected with his and she saw the dull anger simmering deep below their glassy brown surface. It wouldn't be good. She knew that already. He rarely showed her his emotions while still in public. He was furious.

Turning, they headed for the elevators, like any of the other couples eager to return to their cabins to prepare for more feasting. The doors whispered closed, sequestering them into the confined box together and Annie discreetly moved to the end opposite from her husband. Any other time, Victor would have stepped in close to her; it was his way of exerting his dominating power. But Victor didn't move. Leaning heavily against the wall, he tipped his head back and closed his eyes. His face was suddenly pale and sweat rolled down his tensed jaw. "I must've eaten something bad."

Annie watched him warily. He never let anything go that fast or without its measure of violence. And then the doors parted and Victor pushed off the wall and headed, with purpose, to their small windowless cabin. He liked to be certain no one would hear her yells.

As a younger bride, she had tried to run and hide, hoping the anger would pass with time. But the beatings were far more severe than if she followed meekly and submitted to him. At least she could walk away from those.

She breathed deeply, trying to hide her terror, and stood looking at the floor while Victor fumbled with the key card. The door opened heavily and he grabbed her wrist and yanked her into the room, throwing her at the bed like some used up rag doll. She bit her lip to keep quiet and allowed her body to flop on the bed. She had learned long ago that if she relaxed, the landing was always better. She closed her eyes and tried hard not to anticipate the first blow. But it never came. She waited, breathing evenly. Quietly.

Victor groaned and Annie opened her eyes. He stood swaying on his feet, clutching his belly. And then he collapsed in a heap on the floor. She waited a few seconds longer, wondering if it was just another game he was playing, toying cruelly with her emotions yet one more time.

The groaning continued and she sat up and looked at her husband's prone form. His shirt was completely soaked and he had begun clawing at the neckline. Cautiously, carefully, she moved toward him until she knelt at his side. He opened his eyes and stared at her, the first fear she had ever seen in him clouding the bloodshot orbs. Slowly, she began to loosen his neckline, her own emotions a confused mess.

For forty years this man had beaten and intimidated her. He had always demonstrated through physical force that he was strong and in control. And now he lay on the floor, helpless and silently pleading for her aid. A small war stormed across the landscape of her mind, as she debated which action to take. Reaching out, she felt for his neck pulse. It was weak and fading. If she did nothing and he revived, he'd beat her in retaliation. But she so badly wanted to do nothing.

Annie sighed her defeat and began to unbutton his shirt in an attempt to give him more air. As the folds of his shirt parted, she gasped in horror. His chest was covered with huge weeping sores. He hadn't been sweating. He'd been— oozing. She sat back, afraid of contagion. The whole ship had heard the whispered gossip of the strange illness. But there were only two—now three—who had contracted it. And the other two were dead.

Pulling herself to the bed, Annie thought hard. If she reported this, she'd be quarantined along with the spouses of the other two. Her mind churned, eager to break free from four decades of bondage.

His eyes were locked on hers and she knew he saw her indecision fade to certainty. She smiled at him then, determined to have what he had denied her for so long. With as much tenderness as she could muster under the circumstances, she covered him with a blanket and left the room, intent on reaching the Lido deck before someone discovered his body. One day of freedom was all she wanted. Just one day.

Chapter Nine

"THESE SAMPLES are useless." Dr. Perry O'Connell pulled his tired eyes away from the microscope and, removing his glasses, rubbed life into the dry and itching lids. He'd tried every test possible to draw the elements from the tissue samples, but no matter what he used, it all boiled down to the same frightening answer. Someone had taken muriatic acid—toilet bowl cleaner, to be exact—and destroyed them. They were nothing more than a sanitized collection of mush as far as he was concerned. He turned to an assistant and tossed out a directive. "Sarah, get Special Agent in Charge St. Kitts on the phone. I think this is something a little more serious than an illness."

"ARE YOU CERTAIN they've been tampered with?" James was sprawled across his bed, tucked away in the small cabin near the rear of the ship. The phone was clamped firmly to his ear and he closed his eyes against the swaying of the room. A sudden storm rocked and tossed the ship, making rail-side meanderings all but impossible in spite of the great craft's stabilizers.

Steve St. Kitts' voice assaulted him with its precise tones. "So Dr. O'Connell informs me. He says whoever it was put enough muriatic acid in the samples to render them completely useless. Obviously someone doesn't want us to find out what was in those samples, which very much leads me to believe that our illness is a concocted one. I've got Reese working on the two victims' files."

James sighed heavily, cringing at the churning of his stomach. Hopefully his last meal would stay put long enough to finish the phone conversation. He could hear the rustling of papers and assumed Steve was rifling through a file chock full of forms. The urge to gag kept James from cutting in on his boss's monologue.

"Let's see here. Both of them were in active service in Nam between the years of 1965 and 1969 before being posted to other theatres. Reese got a copy of their service files and found that they had both been sent back over in the second wave just after the Tet Offensive. The General was involved in the deployment of a special unit in the Air Force and Ms. Harris was a nurse in a medic unit for—get this—his special forces. It's possible they met. I'll get Reese to dig deeper."

James frowned. So maybe they did meet. But the addition of Victor LeBlanc to the list of victims completely destroyed any Vietnam link. Swallowing hard, he voiced his thoughts. "Reese's information might be a waste of time anyway—as I would have told you if I wasn't fighting my own war against motion sickness."

"Why do you say that? It's the only link that's worth pursuing."

"Yes, sir. It *was* the only link between the General and Mrs. Harris, but our latest victim has never been in the service, much less Vietnam. I did, however, stumble onto a more recent connection."

"Excuse me? What *next* victim?"

James slowly pushed himself up into a sitting position, keeping his eyes squeezed shut. "I was just going to call you when you phoned me. We've had a third victim. Named Victor LeBlanc. You were out, so I had Sylvia run a quick check on him. She was supposed to tell you. He was a vacuum cleaner salesman—and salesman of anything else that can be sold door-to-door. You might want to have her do a more in-depth search. He didn't strike me as the military type. Just a loud mouthed bully from what I saw of him and what his wife shared with us. We've got her sedated and isolated. She didn't take his death well at all. Got rip-roaring drunk and then wanted to throw a party."

The phone went quiet suddenly, and then, from a distance, James could hear Steve paging Sylvia. He smiled a grim smile. While he didn't really like ratting out anyone, Sylvia usually seemed to invite it. Her sarcasm at his request had made it plain that he was clearly inconveniencing her—but that was Sylvia. Julie had chided him more than once for his lack of patience with the older woman, reminding him that not everyone had an idyllic childhood like him. James' stomach rumbled suddenly and he took another deep breath, blowing out slowly. If the chief didn't get back on the phone soon, he'd be visiting the close confines of the bathroom right along with James.

"You still there, Benedict?" Steve's voice cut into his nauseated musings.

"For the most part, sir."

"Sylvia just saved herself a royal reprimand. After you called she did an all-out search on this fellow. Sometimes I think the woman's part blood hound." James reserved comment. "You're right. This guy has no military background. So much for the Vietnam connection. According to this the guy's a poor money manager. He's up to his eyeballs in debt. Poor cash intake. I don't get it."

James opened one eye, watched the walls shift for five seconds and closed it again. "That's what I was going to tell you. I talked with LeBlanc's wife and she said they won their trip on board. It didn't take me long to follow that line of thought and I've already confirmed it with the spouses of the other two victims." Silence greeted James once more.

"You just seem to have all the luck, don't you, Benedict?"

James could hear the amusement and he snorted a reply. "I guess so. Would you mind if I shared this luck with some of the other guys in the Bureau? I'm getting a bit tired of being so lucky."

Steve chuckled. "I've got to say, it's more of a connection than the Vietnam lead for sure. Since you're doing such a fabulous job, why don't you head down to the Captain's quarters and find out if there are any others who've won this lottery or whatever it is? There may be more, and if there are, they could be potential victims. You can give me the names when you get them and we'll continue the search for any other links from here."

James groaned as his stomach heaved again.

"Benedict? Are you alright?" Steve sounded worried.

"Oh, it's nothing a bit of motion sickness medicine won't cure. I just wasn't smart enough to get some before the ship starting bobbing around like a cork in a washing machine. Now I can't get off my bed."

"Are you sure that's all it is?"

James chuckled then. "Yah. I've had it for the past four hours and no boils or sweating has started. So far so good. I'll call down to the medical offices and see if they can send something up. Once I can stand again, I'll go visit the bridge."

"Sounds good to me, James. We also need to get Dr. O'Connell another batch of samples and make sure no one messes with them. Once you get the list of winners, get one of the ship's officers to start interviewing them and the spouses of the victims. They might know something we're missing."

James lay back down and took a deep breath. "I'll get right on it, sir."

A dry chuckle came through the cell phone. "I hope you're feeling better soon, James."

"Yah, me too. I'll keep you posted, sir."

~Chapter Ten

TIP DIDN'T KNOW what to do. There were still several others on the list and he was running out of time. He would have to act quickly and not risk interaction with the victims before they died. That was too bad, because he took intense pleasure in seeing comprehension enter their pain filled eyes as he told them the "who," "how" and "why" of their deaths. He would also miss sharing with them, in those last paralyzing moments, who the next victim would be, knowing they could do nothing to stop him or warn that person. It did, however, free him to bypass the order on the list and jump to one person in particular that he would take an extra amount of pleasure in killing. He smiled, pleased that it was his night to serve drinks before the evening show in the main theatre. It would be a show they wouldn't forget.

The cordial greetings and jovial smiles flowed easily as Tip manoeuvred through the milling crowds. Patrons shuffled their way to the plush chairs lining the theatre, their voices mingling to create a steady hum. He carried his tray of champagne flutes with practiced care, keeping it high above his head and hoping no one would stop him and request a drink. He kept his eyes focused on one man in particular and made a steady beeline for the tall retired soldier.

Tip didn't really care that the aging Northern Vietnamese officer had assumed a new identity and, using his family's substantial holdings, immigrated to America. He had spent his entire life quietly tracking the man. The commanding older gentleman could have undergone cosmetic surgery and Tip would still have found him, so intense was his desire for revenge and his meticulous scrutiny of everything pertaining to the man.

He could still see him, even now, in his mind's eye, decked out in full army regalia, assault weapon cradled in the crook of his arm, eyes cold and unfeeling as a younger Tip was herded from his village. What had moved the Viet Cong leader to release the children, he would never know. But in Tip's mind, it would have been better had he stayed and faced the same fate as the adults.

While Tip was scrounging for his very existence, relying on the tender hearts of the American soldiers for every scrap of food he ate, his enemy looted his homeland and defiled his peoples' remains. Did the man honestly think that a mere name change and move would protect him from those who would never forget? Tip pasted on his smile then, and approached the taller man, pulling a drink from his tray.

"Good evening, Mr. Wong. Are you enjoying your cruise?"

The older gentleman smiled and nodded his answer, receiving the drink with a brief thank you. Tip waited for the

first sip and then wished the man a good evening and
moved on to his next target. "Nam" would understand his
own need to eliminate what Tip considered his own "pri-
mary target." And now that his parents were avenged, he
could die a happy man.

"IT'S GETTING OUT of hand and I can't do anything from
here. I've got no access to files. I have to wait for a phone
call from Steve to get any information. Even Reese is keeping things under his hat. Says I have to go through Steve. I
guess I deserved that one, though, since I basically did the
same thing to him." James knew he sounded frustrated, and
that wasn't exactly the mood he had wanted for his nightly
phone call with Julie. But he also knew that she wouldn't
have appreciated him pretending there was nothing wrong.

"What does Steve think about it?" Julie's voice had
taken the tone she sometimes used with her patients—gentle, prodding, soft.

James sighed and ran a distracted hand through his dark
hair before answering with resignation. "He thinks I can do
more good from here. He says we're lucky to have an agent
on board. Easy for him to say. He's not the one that could
get sick—and this is an illness I would really rather forego. I
know he's right, but it doesn't make it any easier for me. I
guess I just need to be patient and hope and pray for some
breaks."

"Did the most recent victims—were they related in any
way?" Julie continued her questions.

"I'm not sure how much I should tell you without getting the same reprimand Reese got." He sighed. "But I can

tell you that we thought there *was* a Vietnam War connection at first. Since it's no longer viable, I don't think I'll get in trouble for telling you that. In answer to your question—yes, they were related. I think I'll leave it at that, though. I don't need you getting into trouble any more than me."

"James, please be careful. I really do want you to come home from this cruise. And don't get so focused on one solution that you miss out on other things."

"Such as . . ."

"Such as, Why aren't the spouses sick?"

James brought his gaze down from off the distant stars to strain into the inky dark toward the sound of a pod of dolphins splashing near the ship's port side. The lapping water relaxed him and he smiled. "That thought has been rumbling around in my grey matter, but I have to admit I did kind of dismiss it. You're right. I can't overlook other possibilities. Once again, the good doctor has saved me from myself. Did I ever tell you that you're amazing?"

"Not yet, but I suppose it's inevitable."

James choked back a laugh and turned the conversation over to the discussion of her day. "So how is your work going with Cassandra?"

"Not as good as I'd like it to go." Her voice lost its cheery note. "Her parents tell me she screams half-way through the nights and she has to wear a diaper for now. The slightest sounds or gestures from some men make her void. The poor child. She's still not talking, but she did take the teddy bear I bought for her, which tells me that she's starting to trust me a bit more. We've been focusing mainly on the picture therapy, and I cry after seeing some of the things she draws. It's times like this that I hate what I do. I know it's only been a week since she started her therapy sessions, but I was hoping she would have started to open up a bit more by now. I'm running out of ideas." Julie had been actively involved with the child right from the moment she had been rescued a month earlier. She had hoped that the brief encounters prior to the sessions would have been enough to lay some groundwork with Cassandra.

James switched the phone from one ear to the other. "I have an idea: why don't we pray about all of it right now? Everything. Neither one of us should be carrying these kinds of burdens. We both know who's far more capable." As soon as the words were out, he knew they were the right ones, and he continued on before Julie even had time to answer. "Dear Lord Jesus, we come to you with hearts heavy and confused. Both of us are struggling to bring justice to a world gone mad and we both need to remember that you are the ultimate judge.

"God, I bring little Cassandra before you. You know the unspeakable things done to this child by a man who deceived her and would have destroyed her had you not intervened. We thank you for that intervention and ask for your help again. This child is broken and hurting and Julie is struggling to find the right words to bring the suffering to an end. Lord, guide her and help her to do just that. Open this child's heart to your love and use Julie as a witness and an instrument of healing.

"I also lift my case up to you. God, something awful aboard this ship is killing people and I need your help to find a way to stop it. There are things that I am missing and I need to see them. Open my eyes and my mind to what you would have me find. Help me to stop these horrible deaths.

Help me to rely on you in this time and help me to turn over to you my anger against those who take pleasure in hurting others. In Jesus' name we ask, Amen." James opened his eyes and felt the release of burdens too large to ever carry on human shoulders.

"Thank you. I needed that too." Julie paused. "Another thought just came to mind. Have you talked to your friend Sandy Harridan? I know Steve has, but have you?"

"No, but maybe I should. It's probably a good idea. And Julie—thanks. I needed to talk more than I realized."

"Don't worry. You didn't say too much. It's all stuff I have clearance for and I'm going to have a chat with Steve. You need an outlet."

James frowned. He loved being able to have the freedom to talk to Julie, but it rattled him when she started to see him as a patient. It crossed lines that he wasn't comfortable with. "I'll be fine. I don't need a doctor, Jules. I need a friend. Let's keep Steve out of this, ok?"

"I'm not making that promise, but I won't turn it into a professional thing if that's what you're worried about."

He could hear her injured tone and decided it wasn't worth the fight. Sighing, he switched the phone back to the other ear. "Ok. I'll call you tomorrow. Goodnight, Jules." And then she was gone, leaving James to ponder, once again, the complexities of their relationship.

~~~~Chapter Eleven

"I REALIZE I should have come to you sooner, but to be quite honest, that is a part of my life I'd just as soon forget." Retired military scientist Ivan Demensky sat fidgeting in the leather chair. Around him stood a small cluster of stern faced men and women decked out in the white and brown uniforms that identified them as ship's personnel.

Security Officer Mick Lang settled himself in a chair opposite the old man and adopted a gentle tone. "The important thing now is that you *have* come to us. Perhaps you wouldn't mind repeating for Captain Van den Breck and Special Agent Benedict what you told the Chief Officer and me."

The lean white-haired elder smiled timidly up at the ship's security officer through bottle cap glasses and continued his tale at the Commander's nod of encouragement. "I knew General Karl MacCollum by reputation only. I was a scientist working on different chemicals for the army and his name came across my desk often enough. He was one of the men responsible for the defoliation of Vietnam. Our organization researched a variety of chemicals with the idea of clearing land for our soldiers. As you know, Vietnam cost us the lives of many of our boys and we wanted to find a way to keep the enemy from surprising and decimating our troops.

"The General was assigned to a series of missions and rumour had it that he took great pleasure in 'getting even' with the Viet Cong. As to Ms. Harris, I never knew her, Mr. Wong or Mr. LeBlanc. I did recognize their symptoms, however. They showed signs of acute TCDD poisoning. I would recognize those symptoms anywhere. Heaven knows I faced them enough in my work during those years in chemical research."

The ship's Commander reached for a chair and settled into it, a look of confusion crossing his face. "TCDD poisoning? I'm not familiar with it. Would you care to . . ."

"Tetrachlorodibenzo-para-dioxin—a nasty chemical by-product caused by the combination of 2,4-dichloro-phenoxyacetic acid and 2,4,5-trichlorophenoxyacetic acid. Captain, these people all exhibit signs of severe exposure to Agent Orange." The old man sighed heavily. "I knew that someday this would come back to haunt me. God forgives," he allowed his gaze to meet the Captain's, "but he doesn't always smooth things over, now, does he? It appears that someone has resurrected one of our most shameful weapons from the past and decided to use it against us."

Chief Officer Susan Day tossed an alarmed glance at Security Officer Lang and cleared her throat, bringing her own question into the heavy discussion. "But how is that possible? Is it that easy to create such a weapon?"

The weary scientist sadly nodded his head. "If you have the resources, it isn't that difficult. Allow me to explain." He pulled himself to his feet and began a slow shuffling pace from his chair to the large paper-covered desk. There, he scooped up a pen and began to scribble a collection of numbers and letters on an abandoned scrap, hoping to show as he told. "It requires one to have access to a lab and two key chemicals—herbicides, actually. During the war, we discovered that two broad leaf herbicides—2,4-D and 2,4,5-T—when combined, made a powerful foliage stripper. It simply requires a 1:1 ratio of these compounds in their ester form and you have, in essence, Agent Orange. Someone with the right resources would have no problem acquiring the ingredients, I'm sure."

He set aside the writing tool, folded his hands behind his back and took on a teacher's stance while continuing his brief lecture. "The Air Force used C-123K Provider aircraft to spray the fields and jungles of Vietnam. Once the chemical hit the plant, it triggered tremendous and uncontrolled growth in the plant cells. This unbridled growth was the very thing that killed the plant. For years, this spray was used in agriculture to kill broad leaf weeds. It didn't seem to affect the crops in their early stages and it was used carefully under a controlled situation. I wish I could say the same for Vietnam. They were the enemy. They were killing our boys." The old man sighed again, his regret evident in his tone.

"No one would listen to us when we told them about the negative effects on humans. They had a war to fight and General MacCollum was keen to fight it no matter what the cost. My colleagues and I were idealists then—and foolish. We believed in the good of the cause. But when we began to experiment on some of our lab animals, we discovered some of the more hideous side effects.

"Chloracne, birth defects, respiratory disorders and just about every cancer you can name started appearing in our small furry subjects. To my shame, I remained quiet. And because of my silence, many suffer even today. But God is just. I, too, am facing the consequences of my actions. This cruise was a welcome distraction to my recent diagnosis of Hodgkin's disease. Or so I thought. And then I saw the General when he was taken away on deck. His chloracne had only begun but I knew it nonetheless. One can't see something like that day after day and not . . ."

Another uniformed woman burst into the office, her fear and frustration clearly etched across her tanned features as she addressed the Captain. "Sir, we need you right away. We've had another passenger collapse. A Dr. Coleman. He's got the same symptoms."

Dr. Demensky's face grew ashen as he plopped back into his chair, all signs of the lecturer gone. A veined and gnarled hand lifted in a gesture of helplessness and then rested against his temple. "Dear God! Not Kelly! Captain, I knew this man. We came aboard together when we realized we had both won free tickets. He worked in the same lab as I during Vietnam. O dear Lord, have mercy."

Tears of grief began to course down the weathered cheeks as the old man mourned the sudden illness of his associate and friend. The Chief Officer dropped to Dr. Demensky's side and wrapped an arm about the frail shoulders, lifting her frightened eyes to those of the ship's Security Officer. He could see in that look what all in the room were thinking. This was no mere illness. This was a deliberate and focused attack on key people. And it was beyond frightening.

~~~~Chapter Twelve

D R. PERRY O'CONNELL puffed his way down the marble tiled halls, his heels clicking a quick staccato as he passed office doors and other hallways. He knew his destination and his eyes were pinned on the heavy wooden door at the hall's end bearing the name *Special Agent in Charge Steve St. Kitts.* Several sheets of paper fluttered in the doctor's hand as he nearly ran the distance of the hall, and then he was there, tapping on the hard wood surface.

"Come in, Perry." Steve rose and moved from behind his desk to offer a welcoming handshake. "What was so urgent that you couldn't tell me over the phone? Ah, I see you have the test results. Have a seat." Steve took the proffered papers and scanned them while Dr. O'Connell caught his breath. After a moment's silence, Steve raised worried eyes to the red-faced man before him. "Do you realize what this means?"

The doctor nodded, his double chin wobbling with emphasis. "This is no mutation of a normal virus. This is a full blown human-designed toxin. A variation of Agent Orange, to be precise—but a much deadlier and faster acting variation."

Steve let out a soft whistle and shifted through the papers once more. "Well, you'll be happy—or maybe not—to know that we've heard from the ship and a passenger by the name of Doctor Ivan Demensky verified the cause of death: acute dioxin poisoning. And our body count is now up to five people. All but one is linked to Vietnam. Agent Orange . . . hmm . . . an uncanny coincidence, wouldn't you say?"

Dr. O'Connell had leaned forward at the mention of new victims and pushed his half glasses back up the bridge of his nose. "Five victims? Would you care to share what you've got, or is it above my clearance level?"

Steve snorted and tossed the sheaves of paper onto his desk. "Perry, you're part of this, so I'm not going to keep anything back. James has had an interesting few days, to say the least. The samples you got were from General Mac-Collum and Mary Anne Harris, as you know—both involved in the Vietnam War. Then we had Victor LeBlanc die and that's where we discovered the true link. James found out that all three had won a free cruise. And then two more passengers died—both cruise winners. That's where we got pulled back to our initial belief that this has something to do with Vietnam. Number four was a gentleman registered by the name of Mr. Wong, but his real name was Chow Hyang."

At the mention of that name Dr. O'Connell leaned back into the chair, a shocked look on his face. "As in *the* Chow Hyang—slaughterer of whole villages, head honcho of one of the nastiest Viet Cong units in the whole war? I thought he was killed."

"So did the rest of us. And he would have been buried as Mr. Wong, had it not been for a slip of paper tucked neatly into his suit pocket. It was handwritten, declaring the true identity of Mr. Wong with enough evidence to convince us of the truth of it, and included a nice little epitaph that said *now I am avenged*. Shortly after Chow Hyang's death, a scientist named Dr. Kelly Coleman died. You'll love this. He was one of the three scientists on board who actually manufactured Agent Orange for the military—incidentally, the other two were cruise winners too. Nice, huh?" Steve picked up a paper clip and began to absently unravel it as he waited for Perry to absorb all he'd said so far.

"This Doctor Demensky was one of the other scientists?"

Nodding briefly, Steve tossed the mangled paper clip aside and shoved agitated hands into his dress pants pockets. "Yes. He saw the General get sick and knew right away what caused the sores and the sweating. It has taken him the past few days to come out of the closet on this, but he finally approached ship's security and confessed to having been part of the program. Said he came on board with Dr. Coleman and was surprised to see Dr. Peter Drake on deck. When passengers starting dying, his conscience bit him. He identified the General—seems he worked at a distance for him—and the other two scientists. Didn't know Chow Hyang or Ms. Harris but that's no surprise. He also doesn't know Victor LeBlanc—he would have been our one puzzle piece that didn't quite fit if James hadn't had an in-depth conversation with Victor's wife."

"So what now?" Perry pulled at an ear lobe as he stared at the bundle of papers on the desk.

"I have Reese looking into the ship's passenger list to find out who else won and if there are more Vietnam connections—or any connections, for that matter. He's going through passenger manifests for any and all Vietnamese passengers. And then there's the staff. Ninety percent of them are of Indo-Asian heritage, so we could have a perpetrator—or more than one—amongst the crew. There's one good side to all of this, though." Steve wandered over to the window and looked out over the darkening city.

"Oh? What's that?"

"We don't have to worry about an epidemic on board ship."

Perry stood to leave. "No, Steve—but you do have a killer on your hands. You might want to remind James of that."

Steve let out an explosive breath and spoke to his reflection shadowed in the tall window. "He already knows, Perry. He already knows."

~~~~~

"ARE YOU CERTAIN you can't get to them?" The man listened intently to the voice at the other end of the secure cell phone. The clop, clop of the Quarter horse's hooves provided a sleepy backdrop to his anxious conversation and he allowed the large red dun to have his head. The animal relaxed into the gait and followed the trail through the tree-covered terrain that led away from the chaotic city of Los Angeles and deeper into the quiet respite offered along the inclines of Mt. Lukens.

The man hunched into his sheepskin coat, glad that he had brought it as the cool winter rain splashed against the smooth tan covering, leaving darker freckles. The temperature could drop quickly in the higher altitudes and he was far enough from civilization that cold and wet was not something he wished to be. His cowboy hat was jammed tightly onto his head and he was grateful for the warm felt as the water beaded against it and rain off the back. "So who has been eliminated, then?" He listened to the list of names and smiled to himself. Over half of those on Tip's list were dead or in the infirmary on board the cruise ship.

"Good. Good. You've done well, my friend. Don't worry about the others. We can finish what we've begun another time. At this stage in the game, no one can really connect them. Maybe it's just as well if the work is left unfinished for now." He lifted the reins to cue the horse to lighten up on its front end. The animal had a tendency to drop its head so low that it would stumble, and he didn't need a tumble from the saddle any more than he needed a cold.

"Keep me posted, then, and I'll let you know if you should proceed with the remaining subjects." He snapped the phone shut and clipped it to his belt, drawing in a deep breath of mountain air. Enough of his enemies were dead. It should have given him more satisfaction, but he couldn't enjoy the victory yet. He couldn't rest until they all paid for their sins. The taste of vengeance was sweet, but as yet, it was incomplete. The older he got, the more he was learning about patience. It would all happen in time. He just needed to wait long enough.

Chapter Thirteen

"CAPTAIN, WE'VE GOT a call going out from someone aboard ship." Captain Van den Breck left his chair and moved in behind the Communications Officer's shoulder.

"Satellite?"

The young techie nodded and tapped the keyboard. "Yes, sir. Someone has a pretty sophisticated connection. It's loaded down with security systems too. I haven't been able to break into it or find the destination. I can't even pinpoint the source on board. It's pretty scrambled and bounces all over the place within a quarter-mile radius."

"Could it belong to Agent Benedict?"

"No, sir. He requested that I keep an eye out for satellite phone calls other than his. For obvious reasons he couldn't give me his cell signature, but he has been cuing me whenever he sends or receives a message. This is someone else and I've tried everything I can think of to get a link on it to find out where it's going to. There. It's gone."

The Captain stood still, staring down at the computerized console. "You'd better let Agent Benedict know. It might confirm his suspicions, although it's quite possible that someone is conducting business aboard ship completely innocently. Still, he needs to know."

"Yes, sir. Do you want me to start tracking it? I've got a few other tricks that might help me find the signature and then I can send it to the San Diego FBI Bureau. They probably have ways of breaking down the security in the system." The Communications Officer swivelled his chair and looked up at the Captain for an answer.

"Go ahead and do that. If it's an innocent business call, they'll find that out soon enough, but if it isn't, we may just help find this killer that he suspects is on board. For that matter, make that protocol for any satellite calls—Special Agent Benedict's included. That way nothing gets missed."

"SO DID YOU get Cookie cleaned up yet?" James wanted to keep the conversation light. He was tired of talking about the new case—his case. All he wanted was a friendly, warm, breezy chat with the woman he loved, and honing in on her favourite subject would be the best way to do it—in spite of the mutual dislike between man and canine.

The cocker spaniel was given her name when, as a pup, she had managed to open and devour a whole box of Oreo cookies. The poor animal spent two days with an unforgettable belly ache and Julie had an unbelievable mess to clean up. And, over the course of the three years since that time, the dog had continued to give her mistress no end of grief and amusement. The latest escapade had been a swim in a newly dug foundation for an apartment complex. A rainstorm the day before turned the dry pit into a small lake of muck and brackish water—the perfect destination for a runaway spaniel. She returned home with her beautiful silky coat filled with chunks of mud and smelling like a swamp. And James had heard all about it that same night.

Now, listening to Julie recount the bath experience, he was glad he had led the conversation in that direction. And he was glad he had fallen in love with a woman astute enough to know just exactly what he was doing, yet go along with it anyway. They both wanted to share their day's work, but not yet. They needed laughter, ease of conversation, comfort first. And so he listened and chuckled while they discussed the rambunctious dog. Forty-five minutes ticked by. The topic changed.

"So has Dex been bothering you yet, since I'm not there to keep him at bay?" James asked the question, already knowing the answer.

"Of course. I don't know why you continue to hang around with a guy that's intent on stealing your girlfriend."

Dexter Tulloch had about as much chance of stealing Julie as the sun had of rising in the west. "What? Besides the fact that I've known him since grade two and he was the only person that didn't say 'beam me up, Scotty' when he heard my name? I'm not too worried about Dex. You have better taste than that. And I don't exactly hang around with him; we just play tennis once a week. And I let him win. It keeps him playing, which keeps me in shape. Just ignore him as usual. Or even better, tell him how wonderful your boyfriend is."

Julie snorted a laugh. "Modest, aren't we?" And then she sobered. "Do you know he's insanely jealous of you? Has been since I've known him."

"It's your fault, you know." James sighed. "If you weren't such an amazing woman . . ."

". . . I wouldn't have attracted such an amazing man. So let's leave it there and I'll keep brushing Dexter off." As the night deepened and the stars decorated the sky with faint flecks of light, the conversation inevitably turned to the day's events. "I wanted you to know that God is answering last night's prayers. I got a response from Cassandra today. She said 'thank you' for the new colouring book. She stuttered her way through it quite badly—it almost sounded like her teeth were chattering—but she said it."

Julie sounded content and happy and James smiled and pulled himself out of the deck chair. In a slow, meandering way, he crossed the abandoned Sky Deck to settle against the wooden rail within the shelter of the plexiglass shield. "I'm so glad to hear that, Jules. I've been thinking about her off and on all day. It's always the innocents who pay the price, isn't it?" He felt melancholy suddenly and hoped Julie wouldn't pick it up in his voice. She did.

"What happened, James? You sound depressed. It's ok to tell me. Steve gave me clearance this morning. He said he'd call you but I guess he didn't get time. I think he's worried about you. I'm not exactly your official psychiatrist but he figured it wouldn't hurt to give you a release. He—and I, to be quite honest—doesn't want you cracking under the stress of being both an agent on the job and a potential victim." The voice was soft and clearly concerned.

"I see." A deep sigh followed. James wasn't sure how to take that tidbit of information and he chewed on it for a moment. "I'm getting tired of sifting through information and trying to decide what I can and can't tell you. I just hope we don't cross lines here." He paused, not sure what he expected from Julie—or what he wanted from her. No answer came. "I'm assuming, then, that he's brought you up to speed on last night's events. We had two more die."

"Steve told me a little bit." The professional detachment had slipped in.

James frowned at it. Tried to ignore it. "We got good news and bad. It isn't a virus—the good news—so we don't have to worry about contagion. But we do have a killer on board—not exactly something to celebrate about either, especially if you're the next victim."

"You must be relieved?"

That was better—a small tremor that indicated her own small relief. "Well, yes and no. An illness can be treated—most of them anyway. A killer, however, has to be hunted, and I guess I'm the only one on board qualified for the hunt."

"I'll be praying."

James smiled a little. "I know, and that's the best weapon I've got right now." He left the rail and plopped down into the nearest lounge chair. Music filtered up to the deck in muted tones from the disco one floor down and, for the hundredth time, he wished he were with her. "I'm thinking of resigning when this case is done. I'm tired of all of this, Jules. I want a wife and family and I don't want to have to worry about whether you're safe or not."

"But I thought you loved the Bureau!"

"I like a lot of the aspects of this job, but I'm not sure it's where God wants me to be anymore. But tonight isn't really the right time or place to throw all of this at you. Sorry about that. I guess I'm just a bit tired and anxious. And I guess I really did need to offload some of this stuff. So will you be telling Steve about that little radical statement I just made about leaving?"

"Do you want me to?"

He sighed and folded an arm behind his head as he leaned back and stared at the stars once more. "I'd rather you not. I don't want him worrying about whether I'm losing my edge. I'm going to finish this case. I have to find this killer."

~~~Chapter Fourteen

"IT'S SUPPOSED TO be a random process. The new casino—The Czar—they have a computer that draws names from the list of the year's hotel guests. The computer is supposed to have all the top-of-the-line safety measures and firewalls you could ask for, but according to Reese, someone has managed to get into it and choose the winners. None of them have ever been hotel guests. Reese can't figure out how it was done and that's a bit frightening."

Steve's voice barked into the cell phone and James had to pull it away from his ear a bit as he answered. "He's our best computer genius." He was surprised. If anyone could crack a system it was Reese. His computer skills were legendary.

"Yes, and if *he* can't figure it out, we're looking at a seriously talented computer techie somewhere out there gone bad."

"So what's the next step?"

"I need you to find the guy on board ship. Track him down. Do whatever you can to catch him. We need some answers. I don't think he's the brains behind it all, but I could be wrong. And isolate those cruise winners. We don't need the remaining ones dead. Once they're in isolation with the spouses of the victims, I want you to get them thinking—anything at all that comes to mind that might help the case—get them to write it down. Understood?"

James snatched up his ball cap and slipped it onto the top of his head as he prepared to leave the cabin to snatch a quick snack at the breakfast buffet on his way to the security office. "I'm already on it, Steve. We've got the winners in isolation and guards posted. Our killer is going to have a tough time getting to Dr. Drake and Dr. Demensky. I don't know how we're going to track this guy down and I don't think the ship should go anywhere until we do. The Captain's been complaining that he needs to either move on with the cruise or return to San Diego. It won't be long before his patience runs out—not that he really has much choice. He doesn't like just sitting here and he's made that pretty plain. In the meantime, we'll just hope our killer tries to make a move on our guests. That's probably our only chance at catching him. Unless, of course, you come up with something on your end."

"And don't think I'm not trying. I've added quite a few agents to the Bureau search engine. We're digging into everything we can think of. I'll keep you posted."

"Oh, and sir?" James hesitated, not sure he should say it. "I don't know whether to thank you or not for assigning Dr. Holding to me. But I did need a listening ear."

"You're welcome."

James could hear the smile.

AFTER HIS CONFESSION to the security officer, Dr. Ivan Demensky had been ushered to a secure office to wait while an in-depth search was done in order to verify all he had said. When his credentials had been checked and he had been given approval, the group of them made their way to the back of the medical centre and the refrigeration unit where the bodies were stored.

He was noticeably impressed with their facility, complete with a morgue and small laboratory. After all, it *was* a floating hotel occupied predominantly by senior citizens. One needed to be prepared in every eventuality. The compact morgue was a pristine room of stainless steel and bleached linen, all smelling faintly of antiseptic—a room not unfamiliar to the doctor.

A feeling of professional detachment settled over Ivan—a by-product of too many years working in a medical environment—as the first body was pulled from the refrigeration unit inset into the wall. He was thankful for that detachment as his eyes fell on the decayed and blue corpse of the General and he swallowed hard.

The man was covered from head to toe with chloracne, a condition brought on from contact—either through inhalation, ingestion or skin absorption—with dioxins. But it was chloracne like none the scientist had ever seen, and he'd seen plenty of it during his years of experimentation. The General was covered with sores and lumps and tumours. Whole chunks of his corpulent flesh were missing, eaten through by the compound's voracious appetite. It was obvious, even to the unprofessional eye, that he had suffered badly in his last hours.

Leaning over the prostrate corpse, Ivan looked closely at the skin across the General's broad expanse. What was left was swollen and inflamed, under-laced with massive bruising. The more severe areas of the dead man's body were covered with whole sections of lesions filled with cysts and pustules that had consumed clear down to and throughout the muscle and bone. It was obvious that this batch of dioxin had continued its nasty work long after death.

One of the medical officers prepared the microscope and tissue samples for the doctor to view and the elderly man gasped audibly, astounded by the accumulation of cancer cells in each tumour-riddled sample. He'd never seen anything quite like it in all his years. Whoever had prepared this particular batch of Agent Orange had increased the toxicity levels by one hundredfold. And whoever it was meant with all their heart to kill.

Ivan pulled his eyes away from the violated tissue and sat back heavily in his chair. "It's unlike anything I've ever worked with. Someone has a very effective and fast acting weapon in their hands and I'm afraid that someone is on board your ship."

"I REALLY DON'T see why we need to be isolated, Ivan. We haven't done anything wrong."

The older scientist gently shushed his wife as they gathered their belongings from the ample closets and drawers of their stateroom in preparation for their immediate move into protective custody. "I'm sure it's just a precaution, my dear. We'll talk about it more once we're in our new accommodations. Nothing to worry about." But worry was all that occupied the gentleman's mind at the moment as he chewed over all he had seen in the medical centre on deck one. He shuddered as memories from the past pushed to the surface, reminding him of the wickedness he had been part of in the name of war, and he breathed a silent prayer to his Saviour for strength.

~~~Chapter Fifteen

"YOUR FRIEND IS an interesting man. Really strange way of talking, though." Steve clipped out his conversation as he scanned yet another bundle of sheets dropped onto his desk by the irascible Sylvia.

"He's always talked like that—ever since university. Kind of like a robot. I've gotten so used to it, so I don't really notice it anymore. I guess I should have warned you." Static interrupted the hollow voice on the phone.

Steve grunted and tucked the instrument into his shoulder while shuffling through a desk drawer for another file. "Just thought I'd tell you that Mr. Harridan has been quite co-operative with his information. He and the Czar Casino owner have had this business arrangement for several years now. Every year they do the same thing. A handful of casino hotel customers win a cruise. Reese has checked into the computer's system and insists it's secure. I'm going to throw another techie on it just to verify. It's not that I don't think Reese is capable, but maybe he's missing something and just needs some help." Steve chuckled. "Your school buddy was appropriately upset about this whole thing. Offered to do whatever was necessary to help. I told him I appreciated the offer and I'd keep him in the loop. Incidentally, his file came up squeaky clean."

"As I knew it would." James couldn't help the smug tone.

"We had to check, James. It would have been foolish not to do so. At any rate, Alexander Harridan is exactly what he seems. Mighty impressive file, by the way. The man is quite a genius." More paper rattled and shifted.

"Yes, he's certainly that. I'm glad he's cleared. Sandy's always been a bit eccentric, but he's no killer."

"So. Moving on. I'm assuming it was your idea to shut down the ship's internet and ship to shore calls for passengers? Smart move. The media would have a feeding frenzy over this one. I got a call from the Communications Officer saying you told him to track any satellite calls. We'll trace those if we can. Any luck on our killer?"

James sighed and took a quick sip of his soda before answering. "Nope. I was hoping you could help me with that."

"No such luck, but we did find some interesting additional information on the toxin. I had one of the guys do a search on the components in our nasty little cocktail and it appears it has surfaced in the recent past. Five years ago, to be exact." Steve set aside his files and took the phone in his hand again. A busy hand strayed to the dish of paper clips.

"Oh?"

"Yes. Hudson Bay, 2001. A Beluga whale washed up on the shores of a small Nunavut community called Hall Beach. One of the families thought it was a blessing from the gods and butchered the animal. They all died after eating it. James—they were all covered in chloracne when they were found. Somebody on the case was on the ball up there. Tissue samples were taken and added to a very thorough investigation. The RCMP has sent me a file on the incident. No witnesses as to how the animal came in contact with dioxin. No clues beyond the obvious. The hide was preserved and showed minimal chloracne sores, but nothing big enough to deter the family. The guys who did the autopsy on the animal figure it had to have been injected. There was one site on the hide that was bigger than the others and the decay had gone right into the tissue about eight inches deep and in a complete circle.

"They did have one of the residents of a nearby fishing village report a helicopter landing in a field outside the village limits. The old boy who made the report, a guy by the name of Johan Stevenson, said that two men were dropped off and the helicopter left. They entered the village and hired a fishing boat to take them out onto the bay. The boat never returned and neither did the helicopter or the two men. A few of the family members of the crew were interviewed but they didn't seem to know anything. It stood out in the old man's mind because he said they never get fancy visitors like that. He swears it had *Agrinoram* written on the side. Agrinoram is an agricultural chemical company based out of New York State that just happens to carry all the chemicals used in the toxin."

Steve twisted the paper clip into a distorted shape, allowing a brief pause while James scribbled down some notes. "Shortly before the incident, Agrinoram reported the theft of one of their helicopters—imagine that. They found it a year later, torched beyond recognition not ten miles from the fishing village. The pilot was found burnt to a crisp—he also sported a nice neat bullet hole through his skull. What a way to die. They figure he was in on the theft but had a falling out with whoever pulled the trigger. The RCMP assumed that the killer had a back-up vehicle hidden somewhere nearby. The chopper showed no signs of crashing. Somebody obviously wasn't happy with a partnership."

"So maybe the compounds were stolen too?" The frustration sounded clearly over the air waves.

"Probably, but we're seriously digging into Agrinoram's past. Maybe we'll find something important. It's a start, anyway. In the meantime, happy hunting."

"Thanks. Same to you."

Steve dropped the phone onto its cradle, tossed one more mutilated paper clip into the garbage pail and picked up yet another file.

~~~Chapter Sixteen

JULIE WAS A bit nervous as she settled the young couple into the love seat nestled in the corner of her office. The office didn't really look like an office. It looked more like a combination of a play room and a school classroom. Painted in bright colours, it hosted a child-sized table scattered with a few colouring books and crayons, large note pads, paint sets and pastels. Festive murals of animals and cartoons covered three walls and a full length chalkboard covered the fourth. Two small chairs, occupied by the doctor and her young patient, were tucked neatly around the short round table. Teddy bears of all shapes and sizes littered the room, as did small cars and trucks, children's books, puzzles and games.

Cassandra sat, her tiny hands folded tightly in her lap, her eyes deadened with internal pain. In front of her Julie had placed a brightly illustrated children's Bible, but the child stared at it without interest. Julie sat waiting—calm, motionless. She gently talked about the pictures on the walls and the toys. Slowly, she shifted her chair closer, hoping to get near enough that her arm would rest lightly against the child's. She knew that if Cassandra pulled away it was an indication that she wasn't ready to move forward in the therapy. Julie would continue then with the play and drawing therapy to gently crack open the little girl's battered heart and mind. She longed for Cassandra to allow that brief touch, but in each of the past sessions the child had cringed and shifted her weight away from her. It would take a miracle for words to reach her if play and touch couldn't, but Julie believed in a God of miracles. A final shift and a silent prayer brought the contact she had hoped for and Cassandra stiffened but stayed put. Julie smiled, relief flooding through her. "I brought you a new book, Cassy. It's a Bible. You know what a Bible is, don't you?"

Julie indicated the book resting at the table's center, grateful that the child's parents were desperate to try anything and had given her permission to use God's word.

Keeping the bond of touch in place, she reached with her opposite hand for the colourful volume. "It's a story about God and his great big love for us. Would you like to know what the person who made the whole wide world thinks about and does?" Again she waited for a moment, hoping for something. A brief nod followed and Julie continued on. "A long time ago, he made the earth and the trees and the sky and the animals. See in the picture, Cassy? See all the wonderful animals? Well, God wasn't content with just that. He wanted friends. Children that he could talk to and walk with."

Julie turned the page, revealing another colourful painting of a man and a woman wandering happily in a lush jungle garden. Immediately, she felt the girl beside her tense and look away. The people wore no clothes and, although nothing indiscrete was shown, she knew the child immediately associated the naked man and woman with her own traumatic situation. Julie continued to read, hoping that the next words would soothe the young girl. "The man and woman had no clothing but that didn't matter because the world didn't know sin. It didn't know shame."

Cassandra flicked her eyes back to the page, not quite looking at the people, but cautiously interested.

"God loved the man and woman and he gave them everything in the garden he made for them. But he told them, 'Don't eat from the tree in the center of the garden or you will die.' But Adam and Eve didn't know what it meant to die." Julie moved her arm ever-so-slightly until skin was pressed firmly against skin. Cassandra never moved.

"One day, the serpent—called the devil—came along and he told Adam and Eve to try some of the fruit. But they said that God had told them not to or they would die. 'Bah. You won't die. God knows that if you eat that fruit, you'll become like him, knowing good and bad. He just doesn't want you to be the same as him.' So Adam and Eve thought about it. And the more they thought about it, the more annoyed they became. Why wouldn't God want them to be like him? So do you know what they did?"

Julie paused, waiting, hoping—and there it was. Cassandra moved her head once again in a brief shake.

"They disobeyed. I bet you know what that is. I do. I disobeyed my mommy and daddy sometimes when I was a little girl. But Adam and Eve didn't have a mommy and daddy. They had God. And they disobeyed him. Carefully, they sneaked to the tree. It didn't look dangerous. And the fruit smelled so yummy. Eve reached up and took hold of one, pulling it from the branches. She took a bite. Oh, it was so good. She gave Adam some and he ate it. A strange thing started to happen as they kept on eating. Eve looked down, and her face turned all red. She wasn't wearing any clothes!"

Julie could hear Mr. and Mrs. Carpenter shifting in the small couch behind her and she hoped and prayed they wouldn't interfere. This child needed to see that God had intended the human body to be a holy and beautiful thing. She needed to learn that nakedness itself was not evil but attitudes and responses toward it could be. She waited, allowing Cassandra to absorb the story, and then her gentle voice picked up where she had stopped.

"For the first time ever, Adam and Eve felt ashamed. They ran and hid, covering themselves with leaves. But God knew. So he walked through the garden, calling to them because he loved them and didn't want them to be afraid of him. Finally, after a long time searching, God found his children. He was sad because they had disobeyed him. He couldn't let them eat from the tree of life and live forever. He loved them too much. If they ate from that tree, they would always live in sin and he didn't want that.

"So he made clothes from animal skins and sent them from the garden to work for their food. But he promised them something very special. God told Adam and Eve that someday, way down in their family line, a baby would be born who would be the Saviour and that, someday, he would make things the way God wanted them to be. He told the first man and woman that this Saviour would die for all the sins in the world so that everyone could walk with God again."

Julie had slowly and gently lifted her arm and placed it along the back of Cassandra's chair, allowing it to touch her shoulders lightly. The child had accepted it and Julie wanted to cry with joy. Maybe this would be the day that Cassandra would let it all go. She gently closed the book, moving slowly, and with the same gentle voice asked a single question. "Cassandra, what do you think of the story?"

The child sat still for a moment longer and then, to the complete shock of all in the room, whispered a brief reply from the curtain of blond curls that sheltered her downturned face. "G-g-g-god saw me n-n-naked. He s-s-s-saw me."

Slowly, Julie lifted her other hand and placed it over the small one clenched in the young girl's lap. She didn't grip, but laid her palm flat, fingers relaxed and open. The smaller hand turned slowly—hesitantly—and laced its fingers into the larger ones, suddenly gripping tightly as though afraid. "Yes, Cassandra. He saw you. And it broke his heart. Because he loves you so very much."

Again the whisper. "W-w-w-why didn't he m-m-m-make it s-s-stop?"

Julie fought back tears as she moved her thumb to softly caress the back of the small hand. "But he did, Cassy. That's why you're here. He used policemen, neighbours and people who researched with computers. He used them all to find you. To give you back to your mommy and daddy. He didn't want you to be hurt. But God loves us so much that he lets us choose. He let that man choose to hurt you—yes. But he didn't want it. He wanted that man to love him back and to be nice to children. Do you know what Jesus said about people who hurt children?" She waited for the shake of curls. "He said it would be better for them to be drowned than for them to hurt a child. That's how important children are to him. But that man chose to disobey. Just like Adam and Eve. And now, he's letting you choose. You can choose to hate. Or you can choose to heal. Either way, God has left you with the same choice he left everyone in the world. You can love him and have him help you, or you can ignore him." Julie stopped then, and waited again.

A single drip of salty water plopped down onto the table in front of Cassandra, and still, Julie waited. And then the child rose, dropped her hand and flung herself to the corner of the room where her parents sat, tears streaming down their own cheeks. And in the arms of loving parents, the little victim of the evil one began the long and strenuous task of pouring out her pain and sorrow.

Julie remained seated where she was, still and quiet, a large smile spread across her face as she watched the early beginnings of healing through her own teary eyes. And in her heart, she offered thanks and praise to her loving heavenly father who had intervened in the heart of a small child.

~~~Chapter Seventeen

J AMES LISTENED CAREFULLY to Julie's impression of Sandy Harridan. With the kind of dark eyes that drew women and thick, black hair, he could be a real charmer if he put his mind to it.

"Certainly isn't a candidate for a college lecturer, is he?"

"No, but other than that, what did you think of him? I still can't believe that you never met him." James shook his head.

"We've only been dating for eight months, James. You yourself said you haven't seen him in over a year. As to what I think of him? He's nice enough. Quite polite, actually. Almost aristocratic, if you really want to get down to it. I'm actually looking forward to getting to know him a bit. There's a certain gentleman that went to university with him that I would very much like to know more about. I'm going to work hard at getting every little tidbit of information about you from him and I'm not ashamed to admit that in the least."

James could hear the smile in her voice and he frowned, unsure what to think about Sandy's offer to take Julie to dinner. She had postponed acceptance until after she had discussed it with James and he squirmed a bit at the thought of giving her an answer.

"So what do you think?"

"What do I think about a friend I haven't seen in a year who just happens to be rich and good looking taking the woman I love out for dinner while I'm away? Is that what you're asking?" He forced a light tone.

"Do I detect a touch of jealousy from a certain FBI agent?"

"Me? Jealous?" James paused and then relaxed at his own stupidity. "Ok, so maybe a little. Honestly, Jules, if you feel like going for dinner with Sandy, who am I to stop you? We're not married. We're not even engaged—yet." James stretched out on his bed, depression suddenly dampening the evening. He'd been looking at rings in the ship's jewellery shop just that day and was now more determined than ever to have one bought before the ship docked back in San Diego. "So tell me again how this dinner date happened." Julie sighed and James immediately regretted the question.

"I told you: Steve set up a meeting with Sandy and he somehow mentioned my involvement. Whether Sandy guessed or Steve said too much—I can't see that happening—who knows? But before I knew it, Steve buzzed and told me Sandy was coming down to meet me. He told me he wanted my professional evaluation of Sandy after we met. I guess he's covering everyone in this case. I told him I'd be more than happy to meet one of your friends from the good old days and that I would tell him what I thought of the man.

When Sandy arrived we chatted for a few minutes and he invited me to dinner so he could get to know 'Jimmy's girl,' as he put it. I told him I'd check my calendar and get back to him with a date." She sighed again. "Do you really mind that much, James? I won't go if it bothers you."

James scratched at his four-day-old beard and closed his eyes, pulling up her face for the hundredth time. "Not really. Just a case of the insecurities. I don't want him sweet talking the love of my life away from me." Silence greeted his answer.

"Do you think so little of my feelings for you, James?" She sounded hurt.

"No. I sometimes think you could do so much better, though. Look, I'm sorry, Jules. I miss you and that always makes me a bit stupid. I want you to enjoy getting to know Sandy. He's a great guy. Just don't blame me for wishing I was there with you. I like being seen beside you. And believe me, someday that's going to become a permanent happening."

"I'm counting on it."

HE FINGERED THE medals for the umpteenth time. It had been a stupid idea to waste the money mounting them. They had stayed in the case against their velvet backdrop for a grand total of one day and then he pried the thing open and removed them. Strangely, it bothered him to see them bottled up in glass and wood. Like they were in a prison. He continued to massage the face of the Gallantry Cross and stared around the room. Dark. Depressing. Close. A hole in the wall. Papers were stacked neatly on the stained and

battered desk. He felt at home here. Safe. Comfortable. In-
conspicuous. Soon his father would be avenged. Soon all of
those who had destroyed his world would be gone and he
could breathe again. He could step out of the darkness into
the light, knowing that this particular collection of people
could never again destroy another child's future.

~~~~Chapter Seventeen

J AMES FELT HIS excitement and apprehension grow as Steve listed off the collection of information the San Diego Bureau had gathered.

"I had five agents scanning through the crew lists. They weren't impressed when I told them to keep checking the names. I don't know how many times they told me there was nothing there. I knew there had to be. The killer had to know the ship and had to know that our lottery winners would be aboard. Only a crew member could have access to parts of the ship that no one else had access to—like the kitchen. We figure that the toxin was administered through food. We got the ship doctor to check the stomachs of the victims and they verified what Dr. O'Connell had guessed. Perry figured there would be very little left of that organ if the compound had been ingested. When they checked it out they found that the stomachs had all taken the brunt of the poisoning.

"So, after numerous searches, one of the guys lucked out with the Indonesian staff. He decided to check into the organization that does the hiring. The guy running the operation was more helpful than we expected—probably had just enough to hide that he didn't want an FBI investigation—and he faxed a copy of the employee records for each Indonesian crew member.

"I tell you, the guys had one colossal collective headache after going through six hundred crew profiles, but they came across one—only one—where the guy didn't originate in Indonesia. Want to hazard a guess as to where he came from?"

"Vietnam?" James tucked the phone against his shoulder to free up a hand to swipe his card lock.

"You've got it. The name he gave the hiring agency was Tip Doog. It's not uncommon to see names like that in the Indonesian staff, so I never thought much of it, but when I skimmed down to place of birth, it listed the name of a small village in Vietnam. He had no Indonesian papers, so he had to show a copy of amnesty papers that had somehow been issued to him. He had to have had a truckload of money to bribe the guy into taking him on—a rich backer, maybe? This hiring agency is usually pretty strict.

"Anyway, when I started doing some cross-referencing, I discovered that it was one of the many villages that our friend Chow Hyang had decimated. Funny thing was, in this particular village, the man marched all the children from it before he razed it to the ground. Never did that before. Never did it after. This Tip Doog's real name turns out to be Sa'ng Phang—and I can tell you it wasn't easy finding his true identity. I've already contacted the ship's Captain and informed him. I asked him to keep the ship's security clear of the guy until you can come up with a way to apprehend him safely. Who knows what the guy could do if he's carrying this kind of toxin on him. Once it's safe to do so, you can question him and find out who he's working with. Handle this carefully, James. I don't need anything happening to you. And it would be really nice to have Mr. Phang's point of view on all of this."

James kicked his sandals off, examining the beginning of a mild sunburn on the tops of his feet. Maybe it was a good thing his phone had interrupted his relaxation by the pool in the first bright sunshine of the trip, forcing him to return to his room for the needed privacy. He wouldn't be much good if he was scorched into immobility. "I'll be careful. Anything else I need to know?"

"Just a few more details. What ties Chow Hyang and Sa'ng Phang to the others is a soldier by the name of Sergeant Roger Spurgeon, born in Troy, New York on December 19, 1942, to a Robert and Maureen Spurgeon. Roger was the youngest of seven and married his high school sweetheart, Michelle Johns, in May of 1962. A year later they had a son, Jeremy.

"Roger was in that special unit of General McCallum's, and when Sa'ng Phang's village was wiped out, Spurgeon kind of adopted the boy. He let the kid hang around the base and shared his rations with him. Sometimes bought him stuff. Kind of became his father. In 1969, Sgt. Spurgeon took a bullet in the leg and was brought into the medical unit where he was placed—here's a surprise—under the care of Nurse Mary Anne Harris—only she wasn't married then, so her last name was Coddington.

"Her initial report stated that Sgt. Spurgeon had been by-passed—his wound wasn't considered life-threatening at the time—in order to tend to some of the more serious patients. From what I could gather, a series of flukes—you know—mismanaged paperwork, bureaucracy, whatever—kept him from getting the attention he needed. Gangrene set in. The little boy stayed by his side and kept the wound as clean as he could, but by the time they discovered the series of oversights, Spurgeon's leg was so infected it had to be amputated just below the hip.

"Mrs. Harris' report was quite detailed and she added a footnote documenting the need for better organization and more staff. But that didn't help this particular soldier. He went home a bitter, broken man. How we connected Tip Doog to Sa'ng Phan was mainly due to Mrs. Harris' record keeping. She had jotted notes about the boy and tacked a photo of him and Sgt. Spurgeon with the report. It was a unit photo and the boy had been included—sort of a mascot. Why she did it, we'll never know—maybe an attempt to get the boy some help or maybe to cover her own back—but it's our first real break here. It's a much younger version of Phang, but there's no doubt it's the same person as the picture in the cruise line file. We ran both photos through the computer to verify bone structure and it came up positive.

"There are indications that Spurgeon continued to support the boy, since Phang mysteriously acquired a small place in the city and seemed to have a rather consistent influx of money for a couple more years. When the money stopped, the boy disappeared. He must have wanted this ship job bad enough to give the agency what they wanted for information. Otherwise, I don't think we would have found him any easier than we would have known that Mr. Wong was really Mr. Hyang without that little note."

James puttered around the small cabin, pulling trousers and a dress shirt from the set of drawers tucked beneath the window. The phone was again tucked into the crook of his neck with practiced ease.

"It all fits so beautifully." Steve went on while James listened. "And then we have Victor LeBlanc. Late husband of a very resentful and angry wife. It seems Mr. LeBlanc wasn't exactly the kind sweet man he tried to lead everyone to believe he was. I've had a few conversations with some of his fellow salesmen and it appears that Victor was an obnoxious loud mouth who took pleasure in berating his wife. One or two even implied that he beat her. Other than the free cruise, we still haven't figured out where he fits in."

"Got any ideas?" A quick pull through his hair with the comb finished James' preparations and he headed for the door.

There was a pause and a heavy sigh as Steve answered. "No, but we're still digging. I'll get the guys to go back to his childhood if I have to. I'll have them pull up any medical or police references and see if the abuse allegations are true. We'll see what turns up and I'll keep you up to date."

Chapter Eighteen

CHIEF SECURITY OFFICER Mick Lang had thought it best to detain Tip discreetly. He would never admit to himself that wounded pride was the motivator behind his decision. Nor would he ever confess that he felt he was more than capable of doing as good a job at it as the FBI agent. Besides, there was no point in causing more alarm among the passengers than was already present with the high drama that would come from letting an outside security force interfere. Any ruffled feathers would easily be smoothed once the man was in custody. So he had sent another staff member to the bar server with the excuse of needing his help in the Diamond dining room's vast kitchen. That would get Tip off the Lido deck and into the confined area of the elevator where the two of them could restrain him if he presented a problem. It was a flawless plan. His own idea. He didn't really need the FBI agent's help. This was his job.

He watched from the rail of the upper deck that overlooked the open pool. He was far enough back to avoid being noticed, but once his man was directed toward the elevators, he could casually descend the spiral staircase to the deck and follow the two of them at a short distance. From there it shouldn't be too difficult. He hoped. If Tip resisted, the crew around the Lido pool had been informed and would offer assistance. And a handful of security staff waited casually in the bar kitchen.

A shiver of apprehension traced up his spine as he pondered the possibility that the Vietnamese bar tender carried some of the toxin on his person. It was highly unlikely, but he certainly didn't want to find out the hard way. Maybe he should have waited for the FBI agent to come up with a plan of his own. Raising his two-way radio to his mouth, he decided it might be the wiser course to abort the mission. But before he could speak the words that would stop his little sting operation, he noticed the subject of his musings entering the deck area. From the opposite corner of the open area the staff member moved into position. Too late to turn back now. If the fates were smiling on him, he'd have a murderer under lock and key. If they didn't . . ."

CLUTTERED TRAY IN hand, Tip pushed his way through the doors that separated the Lido pool from the overburdened buffet. The shushing of the automatic gliders was lost in the buzz of conversation at nearby tables and he drew in a deep breath of sea air. Only two more men left to pay for the atrocities poured onto his country. Realistically, there were far more than seven people involved in the decimation of the small Asian nation, but these seven people were key to him and his benefactor's particular miseries.

He rounded the curving wall that marked the port side barrier of the bar kitchen with the intention of ducking through the swinging wooden doors typical of such an establishment. He scanned the deck, casually making note of the few rotund and slightly roasted forms reclining on deck chairs. The air was warm enough to warrant the ritualistic basting of human flesh, but the pool itself lacked a population. And then he spotted the quick look-away glance from one of his fellow workers. He frowned and turned to another associate, who also watched him and then pretended he didn't.

As he drew closer to the kitchen, a fellow crew member approached from across the deck, beckoning him with a smile. The man's eyes shifted sideways and then skittered back to his face. They lacked the casual emotion that typically accompanied the ordinary greeting. Something was wrong and he glanced back at the two deck waiters. Both had set their trays down and stood watching as he pushed the swinging door open.

He hesitated for only a brief moment as his mind took in the small cluster of security staff waiting ten feet inside the kitchen, chatting casually to each other and the kitchen workers. Stopping, he tried to back out of the kitchen quietly, setting the tray on a counter—carefully, so as not to draw attention. A dish shifted and the clatter stopped the conversation.

A security officer turned, saw his attempted retreat and took a step forward. "Don't do anything silly, Tip. The Captain just wants to talk to you. It's nothing serious and no one's going to hurt you."

But Tip had no intention of being detained. Life had long ago ceased to be important to him and he had made a vow to make those responsible for his family's death pay and pay dearly—all of them. He knew too much to let himself be caught. He would never betray Nam like that, just like Nam would never betray him. Turning on his heel, he sprinted across the deck, his eyes focused on the distant horizon. The small mob poured from the kitchen like bees from a battered hive and the waiter who had paused just outside the kitchen was bowled over. On either side of him, the two deck servers made a vain effort to zigzag through the oiled and bronzing bodies scattered about on the deck chairs. But he was quicker than his associates. A passenger had just come into the Lido restaurant, leaving the sliding doors open, and Tip dashed through them, running hard toward the back of the ship where the second pool and the open ocean lay. Another swoosh of an automatic door freed him to the humid air and the sound of the ship's churning engines.

Reaching the thick aft railing, he planted both hands firmly and in one smooth motion side-vaulted the oak barrier. With a final heave, he pushed away from the hand grip, allowing his momentum to fling him as far away from the ship's rear as possible. The first impact landed him with a solid thump against the dining room's thick glass windows. It was a fortunate thing that it happened between meals, but even still, the dining crew, busy setting tables for the dinner hour, would never forget that sound or the vision of their crewmate smearing his way down two stories of sloped glass.

Had he not pushed so hard, he would have plopped unceremoniously onto the third floor outdoor wooden deck with minimal injury and a lot of questions to answer. But he *had* pushed hard. And so he overshot the deck and snapped his back on the second oak-topped iron guard rail. A sharp pain screamed its way down his spine and then all sense of feeling left him as he continued his downward slide. Upon clearing the slope of the third level, the ship's hull banked steeply inward, leaving the remaining drop an aerial affair. Limbs deadened by a severed spinal chord flailed the air like useless ropes or the cloth-and-stuffing limbs of an abandoned rag doll.

Tip landed hard on the water's surface, having no ability to right himself or break his fall, and the wind was knocked from him as he plunged beneath the salty waves. There was no chance of resurfacing as lungs instinctually struggled to draw in air. Like churning bellows they pulled in great quantities of cold salty water and his head spun as the oxygen burned up. His last thoughts, between bursts of panic, were of his parents' scorched and twisted bodies lying on ground that had for centuries harboured and fostered their ancestors.

~~~~Chapter Nineteen

THERE WERE TWO ways James could deal with the anger. He could bottle it up or he could find a way to vent. His first instinct was to call Julie and rant. Not a good way to foster a relationship. He'd tell her—certainly—but she didn't need to deal with the brunt of his anger. And so, he chose the second way: a golf club on the top deck driving range. As much as he would have loved to whack those little white balls out over the water and watch them disappear in the chop, he would content himself with smacking them at the net cage. And with each drive was a muttered comment. He was glad for the lack of interest—or, perhaps, lack of awareness—that the other passengers had for the driving range. He could release his comments and not be heard.

"Stupid security officer!" Whack! "Did he think he was going to come along quietly?" Smack! "The guy killed five people, for crying out loud!" Whoosh! James swung hard, overshot the ball and almost toppled himself onto his backside. Tossing the club onto a deck chair, he plopped himself

down and took a deep breath. So what if he was acting a bit
juvenile. Leaning back in the chair, he allowed his mind to
run through the past few hours. No doubt the crew was
cleaning the gore off of the dining room windows—maybe
they already had it done. Certainly the Captain would be ad-
ministering a royal reprimand to Security Officer Mick Lang
and his band of merry men, but that didn't make James feel
any better. Steve wouldn't be a happy camper when he
called with the news.

Unclipping his phone, James tossed a glance around and
decided he had released enough anger to face his superior
without saying something he'd later regret. Punching the
speed dial, he hoped and prayed that he would have the patience to be civil to Sylvia.

"Special Agent in Charge Steve St. Kitts' office. How
may I help you?"

Her smoke-scarred voice grated and James mentally pe-
titioned the heavens above for help. "Sylvia, I need to talk
to Steve ASAP. Would you patch me through?" There was
silence. As though she sensed his urgency. Or his anger. Or
both.

The sarcasm was gone and she answered with her most
professional tone. "Certainly. I'll put you right through."
And then she was gone and he was left waiting for a brief
moment.

"James? Sylvia said you sounded pretty stressed out.
What's happened?"

James pulled himself back to his feet, scooped up the
driver and began to pace the confines of the net cage like a
captured beast furious with its confinement. "I hope you're
sitting down, because you aren't going to like what I'm

about to tell you. Our only lead, Mr. Phang, is now digesting in the belly of some aquatic carnivore somewhere in the ocean's depths." He filled in the details, feeling the anger building once again as he recounted the security officer's blatant disregard of orders. Steve remained silent and James could picture him, stock still, as the information was absorbed. Where James showed his anger almost immediately, Steve clamped down on his. It was the only time the man was ever motionless, as though by controlling his movements he could reign in his emotions.

"And does the Captain have this officer in custody?"

"Oh, you bet he does! He's made it quite plain that if we don't deal with this guy, he most certainly will. I took a bit of pleasure in informing Mr. Lang that he had just put himself on the suspect list. He turned a nice shade of green and protested that he was only doing his job and that he didn't know Phang would jump. So now what do we do?"

"Well," Steve chewed on the word. "You go back to guarding those two remaining passengers—just in case—and I'll do some more digging. We've been lucky twice. They say three times . . ."

JULIE CLICKED her way across the mall parking lot. It had been an emotional day and she needed her cocker spaniel, a hearty bowl of hot buttered popcorn and a sappy chick flick to help her unwind. Dexter Tulloch was the last person she wanted to see, and she ducked past a minivan, hoping he hadn't spotted her coming out of the video store. She grimaced as she heard her name called out in that smooth, smarmy way he had.

"Hey, Julie! Wait up!" Dexter jogged to catch up.

He was wearing a form fitting T-shirt and tight jeans and she fought the urge to roll her eyes. "Hi, Dexter. What can I do for you? I thought you knew James was away and wouldn't be playing tennis this week." She hoped she didn't sound as impatient as she felt. It wasn't in her nature to be deliberately rude.

"Oh, I know James is away. I'm not here for him. I'm here for you. Just wondering what you were up to tonight. Thought you might like to take in a movie. You know— keep you company while your man's away." He pasted on his professional smile, the one he used to impress his law clients and whatever lady happened to catch his eye.

"Sorry, Dexter, but I have plans." She continued across the lot, kicking herself for parking her car so far away.

"What about tomorrow night? We've got another week before James is back. I wouldn't want him to think that I'd neglected you while he was gone."

He matched pace with her and Julie could feel her hackles rise. "Dexter, unlike you, I like to have one relationship at a time. So, if you don't mind, I'll just stick to the one I'm in." She refused to face him and stopped at the driver's door, stabbing the key at the lock.

"Yah, but he's not here right now, so technically, you're not in a relationship—at least not as far as I'm concerned." He leaned against the rear driver's side door and folded his arms.

"Well, I *am*, as far as *I'm* concerned, and I guess that's what counts. Now, I'd like to get on with my evening." Yanking the door open, she dropped into the seat and made to pull the door shut.

A hand clamped on the top corner and held the door firm as Julie looked up with a startled expression.

"Someday James is going to move on. He's a career man, Julie. And when he does, you're going to be left high and dry. Let me know when that happens and I'll be there."

He released the door and she slammed it shut and locked it. Her heart was pounding as she stuffed the key in the ignition and turned it. Without looking to see if Dexter had stepped away from the car, she revved the engine and pulled out from her parking spot. And then the anger hit her. *The nerve of the man! Who does he think he is?* She debated the idea of a restraining order but wondered if there was enough to qualify his actions as harassment. Probably not. But James was certainly going to hear about it. It was high time he understood just how determined Dexter was.

~~~Chapter Twenty

I T WAS LATE when the call came in and the man pushed the satin sheets back and snatched up the device. "Yes?"

"The files have been stripped. No one can trace it back to you. You can trust me on that."

Leaning back against the pillows, the man smiled. "Well done. The money will be deposited in instalments, like we agreed, and I think I'll slap a bonus onto the portion that you'll be getting for this one." He paused. "You're certain no one will find them?"

"I'm positive. You are officially clean and the trail should stop cold at Phang. Oh . . . and I'm sorry for your loss. I know you two were close. I appreciate the bonus too, but you know it isn't necessary. I'm in the same boat you are. I thought you understood that."

"I'm just showing my appreciation. You can't fault me for that. And I know exactly where you stand in this. Just keep your eyes open for me, will you? It'll all soon be over. We only have two left. We'll have to wait until they come back to port, but I don't mind the wait. I've waited this long; I can wait a few more days." He waited, knowing that the silence on the other end of the phone was filled with shared memories of past horrors.

And then the voice continued. "Just let me know if you need me. I've got the bogus accounts set up and I think I've left enough bunny trails to keep them busy until it's over. We might just get away with this, you know."

"It's a pleasant thought." He chewed the side of his cheek for a moment. "But I don't really care as long as I have my revenge. Good night, friend. Thanks for your help."

"G'night, Nam. Sleep tight."

"AND Y-Y-Y-Y-YOU'RE sure J-J-J-Jesus loves m-m-me? Even after I let Mr. D-D-D-Deeder . . ."

The question was thrown at Julie in the sweet piping tones of six-year-old Cassandra Carpenter, but Julie cringed at the effort that it took for the child to chutter out the words. If anything, the stuttering had worsened. But she was talking. She was opening up and Julie marvelled at the speed with which the little girl was pouring out her pain. Cassie's parents had stepped back and given Julie free reign. They didn't care if she had the girl chanting mantras about spaghetti noodles, so long as it helped their daughter to heal.

"I am positive Jesus loves you, sweetie. And remember what I told you? You didn't do anything wrong. Mr. Deeder tricked you. There was absolutely nothing you could do that would have changed anything. He lied to you when he said your mommy was in the hospital. He knew all the right things to say. And you knew him and trusted him. You didn't do anything wrong and I'm going to keep telling you that until you believe me, ok?"

Blonde curls bobbed hesitantly. "But if I did want to say I was sorry—just in case I did something wrong—will Jesus forgive me?" She threw a worried look at her mom, who sat quietly in the corner of the office, and received a small smile in answer to that look.

"Yes, Cassie. Jesus forgives us all when we trust him. Did you want to talk to him? Maybe tell him what's bothering you?" Julie had her arm draped about Cassandra's shoulders again and the little girl had snuggled into her. Again the curls answered yes. "Sometimes I just tell Jesus as though he was sitting right beside me and sometimes I close my eyes so I can concentrate better. What would you like to do?"

Again the child looked at her mother, confusion flickering in her blue eyes as she stuttered out her answer. "I think I'll close my eyes. To pretend I'm alone."

"Fair enough. So let's close our eyes and you just go ahead and talk to Jesus. He's listening. I promise." She looked at Mrs. Carpenter's worn face and saw the sorrow there. Julie offered a compassionate smile to the mother, trying to relay to her that it would all be fine, and then she dropped her head as though in prayer.

"Dear Jesus," the voice was quiet—timid—and filled with the staccato of repeated consonants. "Miss Julie says that you always listen. And she says that you always forgive when we do bad stuff. I'm sorry for the bad stuff I did. I went with Mr. Deeder even after my Mommy said I

shouldn't go with people unless they know our secret pass-
word. I'm sorry for hating Mr. Deeder. I want to hate him.
I'm mad at him 'cause he did stuff . . . but Miss Julie says
that hate just hurts me, not him, so I'm sorry for hating
him."

Julie watched through partially closed eyes as Cassie
peeked an eye open to look over at her mom. The child's
face was twisted with anguish and then the eye squeezed
shut again and she continued, the stutter thickening her
speech even further.

"And Jesus . . . I'm sorry for being mad at Mommy and
Daddy. They didn't know Mr. Deeder was bad. Miss Julie
says they would have helped me if they knew where I was.
She says they wanted to help me. I'm sorry I didn't like
them for a little while."

She stopped then and a sniffle interrupted the charged
air. Julie stroked her hair and looked over at Mrs. Carpenter.
The woman's face was contorted in the agony of an incon-
solable loss and Julie gestured subtly for her to come to the
child.

She needed no further urging and rushed to kneel before her daughter. Taking her hand, Cassie's mom wiped at
the tears that had begun to trail down her daughter's cheeks,
her own tears running freely. "Cassie, Daddy and I understand why you would be mad and we really wanted to help
you. We're sorry that we weren't able to. We love you." The
little girl abandoned the child-sized chair and folded herself
into her mother's embrace. Together, they sobbed out their
pain and forgiveness, and again Julie found herself smiling
through blurry eyes.

Chapter Twenty-One

"I'M SORRY, SIR, but that's the best I can do." Reese stood before Steve's desk, frustration written across his face. He cracked his knuckles quietly behind his back.

Steve ran his hand across his wiry hair and clenched his jaw. "So tell me again what you did get." He gestured for Reese to sit, and the older agent settled his bulk into the seat opposite the desk.

He watched Steve carefully as he spoke, gauging the man's nervous energy. "Well, like I said, I went into the hard drive and started looking for trap doors—entry ways into the computer. I have this neat little program . . ."

"Reese, spare me the technical details and just tell me what you've got." Steve didn't lose patience often, but when he did, it was a sure sign that whatever case was in the works wasn't going the way he'd like it to go.

"Sorry, sir. Ok, so I found the trap door, and when I tried to trace it back, a nasty virus was there waiting. It chewed up some of my files and scrambled a few others before I tracked it and destroyed it. It also effectively closed the trap door into the Czar's computer. So I can't track the hacker. It's a dead end, sir." Reese dropped his gaze to the floor as though ashamed of his failure.

The tapping of a pencil against the wooden desktop interrupted the silence as Steve stared out the window, his mind churning. What was he missing? Why were all the doors slamming shut on this case? Pushing out a heavy breath, he turned back to his agent and shrugged. "Ok. So you did what you could. I'll leave this with you. See if you can keep working with that system. See if there's something—anything—that you've missed. Anything new on the personnel files? Find anything important on our victims?"

Reese shrugged helplessly. "I've gone over those documents several times now, but I'll keep checking them if you'd like. Maybe I'm not seeing something that just wants to jump out and bite me." He shrugged again and looked at the front of the desk in defeat.

Steve turned away from the window and looked at Reese for a moment. Heaving a sigh, he nodded. "I'll let you get back to work, then." He watched the fifty-nine year old agent pull himself out of the chair and exit the room. If Reese couldn't fix this mess, who could? The door clicked shut, leaving him alone, and he turned to his intercom. "Sylvia, get me Jonas Taylor. I'd like to talk to him about his findings with the Czar computer. And Sylvia? Don't mention to anyone that he's even involved."

"Yes, sir." The crisp voice crackled through the speaker and then was gone.

Steve leaned back in his chair and folded his hands behind his head. Something wasn't computing, and it wasn't just the Czar's hard drive.

~~~~~~

"WHAT DO YOU mean he made a move on you?" James towelled his damp hair and opened the bathroom door to let the steam from the shower escape.

"I was leaving the video store and Dexter made a move. Asked me out." The bathroom air wasn't the only thing filled with steam. Julie's voice carried a hard edge. "It made me so mad to think that this guy calls you a friend."

Stepping out into the cooler air of the cabin, James flopped onto the bed. "Ok. Calm down and tell me exactly what he said." He could feel his own temperature rising as Julie recited the short exchange she had with Dexter in the parking lot. James raked fingers through the wet mop and started sifting through solutions in his mind, immediately cancelling out the ones involving his service revolver.

"I don't exactly feel comfortable around him now, but I think I've dealt with it."

Julie's idea of dealing with Dexter would have involved some clinical psycho-speak, a warning and if it continued, a restraining order. James wanted something a bit more powerful and a bit more immediate. "I'll call Reese. He'll deal with it. I'll also call Dexter and let him know that you've shared this bit of information with me. Nothing confrontational—just a need-to-know conversation."

"No, James, you won't." The firmness of her voice caught him off guard and he set the towel aside and gripped the phone, ready to argue the point. Julie didn't give him a chance. "As I said, I've dealt with it, and as much as I appreciate the sentiment, I don't need help with this one.

Let's not make it more difficult than it is. If I need you to step in, I'll ask, ok?"

James nodded as though she could see him and offered a grudging, "Ok. So what else is happening in my beautiful girl's world?" He deliberately lightened the tone.

Julie took his change of subject as agreement and moved on. "Cassandra is healing, James. It's nothing short of miraculous to see her. All I can say is keep praying. Her parents sit and listen patiently while I tell her all about the Bible. I'm just blown away."

"Well, they're hurting too. They need Christ as much as Cassandra does. I can't imagine what they must feel. If I were her father . . ." He could feel a nudge of anger again and worked to stay relaxed.

"Yes, I know. They are devastated. I keep telling Cassandra that forgiveness helps her heal. That it's more for her than it is for her abuser. I think that helps her parents too."

"You're a very wise woman, Dr. Holding, which is why I'm going to marry you some day." Tucking an arm behind his head, James stared at the ceiling as his mind worked through what to do with Dex. The conversation wound down and the silences began to stretch out.

"I suppose I should hang up. I really should get some food. Another night with just me and Cookie and a big tub of popcorn." She sighed.

"I'll be home soon. I love you." Her absence hurt.

"I love you too."

The dial tone signalled the end of their conversation and James immediately punched in his partner's number. After two rings the familiar voice bellowed into his ear.

"Reese here."

"Yah, Reese. I'm having a bit of a problem with Dex and I don't want it to look like I interfered. It appears that he's got a thing for Julie and is making it obvious . . ."

~~~Chapter Twenty-Two

"I'LL GET RIGHT on it, sir." Jonas Taylor tried hard not to look like the stereotypical nerd. But red hair and freckles combined with a boyish face and thick glasses didn't help the image. What he lacked in physical attributes, he worked on in style. A tailored pinstripe suit encased the lean framework in charcoal hues. His hair was carefully groomed and he wore a dab of cologne.

As Steve St. Kitt's voice faded away, Jonas hung up the phone, gnawed on the pitted and roughened end of his pen, and swung his chair around to his computer. The clatter of keys occupied the space of his cubicle for some time as he dove into the past of Victor LeBlanc. Why Reese hadn't been able to find anything on him was a mystery. Jonas felt uneasy back-tracking over a fellow agent's work, but Steve had insisted that Reese was missing something. Maybe he was losing his touch. Who knows?

Diving into birth registries, newspaper archives, school records, police files and confidential personal files, Jonas began to unravel Victor's history. Only once was he interrupted by the gentle tones of Dr. Julie Holding as she passed the open doorway. He smiled briefly as her voice carried on down the hall, chatting amiably to the little blonde girl that James Benedict had rescued. The smile widened. James was a lucky man. What Jonas would give to be in his shoes. A frown replaced the smile and he swung his chair back around to the task at hand. If he didn't find the link from Victor to the other victims, James might not be around long enough to enjoy his relationship with Dr. Holding.

Slipping out of his suit jacket, he rolled up his sleeves and continued in his time travel. His discoveries weren't pretty. The older Victor got, the nastier he got. Jonas cruised through a childhood riddled with complaints against bullying on the playground. The teen years were more of the same, with a few misdemeanours thrown in. Jonas pulled up a link that had Victor and Annie's names on it and he stopped. Sitting back, he plopped both hands on the top of his head and whistled low.

"Well, I'll be. Wait 'til Steve sees this."

"AW, COME ON, Reese. I was only having a bit of fun. Like I always do." Reese had caught up with Dexter just outside the courthouse. He was careful not to move in too close, but certainly didn't give Dex much manoeuvring room. The lawyer was decked out in an Armani suit and had just won another round for one of the local thugs. He was trying in vain to slip past the agent and continue down the court- house steps. Reese blocked his path again.

"Well, see, it's like this, Dex. Nobody thinks it's funny. Least of all, Julie, so maybe you should just lie low for awhile." He turned to scan the busy sidewalk.

"Are you threatening me, Reese?" Dex had grown still and Reese snorted.

"Not even close! I don't need some lawsuit coming at me. I'm just warning you that a restraining order wouldn't look nice in your portfolio any more than assault on a lawyer would look good in mine. It's not like this is the first time you've hassled her, and you don't seem to joke about it with James around. One would think that you were afraid James might actually take you seriously. He might not care what his service record said." Reese showed a flash of his big teeth as he pictured the thought.

"James and I have been friends forever. He's not going to take this seriously. I didn't mean anything by it, anyway." Reese pinned him with a look. "Ok! Ok. I'll leave her alone. I get the point. No harm done, right?" Dex held his hand up in surrender and waited for Reese's nod.

Reese stepped back and watched the lawyer scurry on his way. He smiled as a muttered insult drifted back to him. He wouldn't even let James owe him for this one. He'd never liked the snake to begin with. *So much for your tennis games, buddy. You're going to need a new partner.*

JAMES STOOD dripping chlorinated water at the forward rail of the Sea Ward Pool—the third and smallest pool on the ship. He dabbed at his face with a thick towel, trying hard not to get his phone wet. The temptation to ignore the insistent bleating from the pocket of his shorts resting on the deck chair had been strong. He badly wanted this small break to let his mind relax a bit. A chill wind bit deep into his flesh, causing his skin to freckle with goose bumps. Anyone watching would have thought he'd gone insane for swimming in water that had followed the air's dip in temperature. He didn't care. The cold water was just the tonic he needed. Too many hours had been spent churning through all the information he had available, and a quick dip in the pool was needed to clear away the clutter. And then his phone rang. It would either be more information to assimilate or more dead ends. "James here. What's up?"

Steve's voice echoed in his ear and James could hear the fine edge of excitement. "We found the link with LeBlanc. It took some doing, but listen up. He and his wife were foster parents about twenty or so years ago and the children were taken away from them because he had a bit too much of a temper. When the kids were consistently darkening the hospital doors for strange and inexplicable injuries, Children's Aid got suspicious and, after a thorough investigation, revoked the couple's privileges."

James wrapped a towel around his waist, one across his shoulders and a third over his head. He looked like a navy blue mummy. Shivering against the wind, he dragged the deck chair to an empty spot at the rail, scanning the area to make certain no one was close enough to hear before dropping his soggy frame onto the vinyl covering. "Go on."

"After the children were taken away, Victor vented his frustrations on Annie, batting her from one medical facility to the next. I'm actually surprised that he took her on the cruise with him. He had a bit of a roving eye. And it didn't just stop with him looking. Several affairs come and gone and the woman still stuck by him. You've got to wonder at that kind of loyalty.

"Anyway, I had Jonas Taylor contact the Children's Services department to see if they had fostered out a child named Tip Doog or Sa'ng Phang as one of his charges. Since the boy had been supplied with money at one time, we thought he might have had enough cash to get to America. You never know. But no child by that name was in the system. Other than that, we couldn't think of any connection. I had Sylvia send Jonas all files that contained all the names with possible links to this whole thing and he made a overview and printed it out for me, throwing in any additional information he'd found. And that's when we saw the one detail we hadn't really had anyone check into. What happened to Sergeant Spurgeon's son?"

James frowned, trying to recall Sergeant Spurgeon and then remembered he had been Sa'ng Phang's guardian in Vietnam. Subconsciously, he scanned the collection of abandoned deck chairs around him as Steve continued.

"We had Sylvia do what she does best—I'd like you to keep this quiet, by the way. I'm not convinced that Mr. Phang was the only one on board, and I'd rather not let anything out that could endanger you or any more passengers. Sylvia dug deep and discovered that Spurgeon's son, a kid by the name of Jeremy, ended up an orphan—in foster care."

James sat forward, all ears. "Do tell. And let me guess—he ended up in the care of Victor LeBlanc?"

The smile was clear in Steve's voice. "You guessed it. Jeremy was one of the children that spent as much time in hospital as he did in Victor's home. What we didn't know after our initial discovery of Spurgeon's connection with Phang was that a year after Spurgeon's death, Jeremy's mother committed suicide. Never even thought to check into his family—I guess I'm slipping. Anyway, the boy got battered pretty badly. Concussions, broken arms and fingers, cuts. You name it. The poor kid was almost fourteen when he finally hit a good foster home, and this is where it gets interesting."

James left the deck chair, scooped up his things and tracked across the deck to the elevators, listening carefully as he punched the button to his floor. The doors swooshed closed and he dropped quickly, opening again to an empty hallway.

"He actually settled into the new home well and, a year or so later, was adopted by the new family, giving him the name of Jeremy Abrams. The kid excelled in school and was fascinated with the history of the Vietnam War and anything else pertaining to that part of the world. The child welfare records say that the adoptive parents noticed a remarkable change in him for the better after he started writing to a pen pal in Vietnam."

"Let me guess again—Sa'ng Phang?" James opened his cabin door and headed right to the bathroom where a plush terry cloth robe waited.

"Right again. I managed to contact the Abrams family—you won't believe this, but they moved to San Diego when their kids all grew up and moved out—and they still have some of his belongings. He hadn't shared the letters with them but there was one still in a shoe box in his bedroom. They had been able to get it from his school locker. They said it was written in broken English and signed *S*.

Phang. I'm driving over to visit with them personally this afternoon."

James schooled his facial features to hide the surprise. It was an instinctual response. "Don't you have somebody else to do the job?" He paused then. "You're not telling me something. What's up, Steve?"

"I'm not sure myself, but I think I'm going to get a bit more involved in the hands-on areas of this case until my instincts are satisfied. So anyway, Jonas turned up a few other small details that give us a tentative perpetrator. Jeremy did a huge science project on our favourite chemical compound—Agent Orange. He got top marks for it and it seemed to be the boost he needed because his grades suddenly shot to the top of the class. By the time he finished his high school years, he had several scholarships lined up offering to pay full tuition for first year of university. He jumped at the opportunity and filled his first year with every course imaginable in chemical science, biological science—anything that had to do with science at all. And he aced the courses with top marks. Unfortunately, he went a little too far in the lab one day and actually concocted a batch of Agent Orange—or something close to it. He sprayed some of the lab pets with it and they all died. It was a nasty way to end such an excellent academic year."

James could hear Steve's heavy breathing, a true sign of excitement and a rare occurrence. "So I guess you're going to go find this Jeremy Abrams and have a few words with him?"

Steve cleared his throat and hesitated, the excitement dying as quickly as it had come. "This is where we've run into a bit of a problem. After his first year at college, Jeremy Abrams ceased to exist. That summer, while messing around in his basement lab, he mixed the wrong chemicals and blew up his adoptive family's home. They found his body scorched beyond recognition. It was a bit disappointing to find that out because I was pretty sure we had our man. It's a good thing he hadn't cleared out his locker yet or we wouldn't have had access to the letters. The only thing I can think of is that Sa'ng Phang took up where Jeremy left off. As to finding a backer, maybe he found someone who had a similar experience. Got any suggestions as to where we should go from here?"

The grumble in James' stomach interrupted his concentration and he grabbed an apple from the fruit basket on his bureau and bit deep. Chewing quickly, he spoke around the juice and pulp. "Short of going through all the files listing soldiers with medical problems due to Agent Orange, I get the feeling we're at a dead end again. Yes?"

Steve grunted a reply, obviously not happy that James didn't have an answer for him. A moment's thought allowed James to finish the mouthful of apple. "So what did the autopsy find? I'm assuming they got a dental records match to verify the remains?"

"Well—they actually couldn't do a positive ID." James could hear papers rustling. "Let's see. The report says here that the ID match was not conclusive. They couldn't find the head. There's a blurb here written by the coroner. He had an explosives expert come in and examine the corpse. The expert agreed that, based on the tissue damage, the head must have exploded in the blast. Jeremy must have had his face pretty close to those chemicals to completely annihilate his skull. So there really was no positive identification on the corpse."

James could hear the scepticism and he followed the train of thought. "It would be a really good way to disappear without dying—you know—find a body, blow up the head. And if my guess is right, that's what you're thinking—yes?"

"It's too bad we couldn't verify it. Unless . . ." Steve stopped.

"Unless you compared medical records from Jeremy's many hospital visits to the fracture scars on his arms and hands." James finished Steve's thought. "You think the kid faked his own death?" It was a chilling thought.

"It did just cross my mind. And if a college kid can make himself disappear in such a violent way, he could be equally capable of tracking down all those he felt were responsible for the death of his father—and mother, too, I guess. We've got our motive.

"Now we just need to find Jeremy. If he staged his death, then he had to find a new life—a new identity. And you and I both know how easily that can be done. But we're getting ahead of ourselves a bit. First, I have to meet with the Abrams. I'll try to convince them of the necessity of exhuming the body. I'll get forensics to do a complete examination on his arms and hands. If the fracture lines on the X-rays match up with the calcium deposits on the bones, that will give us a positive enough identification and it will shoot this whole theory in the foot. But if it doesn't match . . ."

"So what do you want me to do?" James was now sitting on the bed and working another piece of apple around his words.

"I'm going to get in touch with the Captain and get the victims' bodies released. Dr. O'Connell needs them here to do a proper autopsy on them. I'll need you to oversee the operation and make certain that no one comes in contact with them. We still don't know if the compound is strong enough to spread through skin contact. Oh, and get all the vials gathered up that you found in Sa'ng Phang's room— and any other evidence. We're also going to have to escort the Security Officer ashore. We need to question him. I'll impress upon the Captain the importance of full co-operation. I don't imagine you'll have much trouble. Anything else?"

"No, sir. I'll get things worked out from this end."

~~~Chapter Twenty-Three

FIVE BODIES ENCASED in thick black plastic rested in a tidy row on the ship's Sky Deck. The warm winter air churned and whipped with the rapidly turning rotors of the larger military chopper. For the second time, a man fast-roped his way down to the isolated weather-bleached deck and its small collection of sombre-faced witnesses. Several security staff stood near the double stairs, keeping the area free of curious passengers while the medical personnel waited for the body basket to be lowered. One by one, the remains of the victims were secured and retracted into the belly of the large bird until the deck was empty of its morbid collection. An FBI agent in full gear stood next to Special Agent James Benedict as a dishevelled security officer was ushered, handcuffed, to the deck. A harness was slipped onto the man and he and the new agent were clipped to the dangling rope and hauled up as the last course for the huge bird's unusual meal. With that final extraction and the crisp whipping of air currents, all evidence of the journey's violence was gone. The curious onlookers that lined the upper and lower promenade decks and the various pool decks slowly trickled away, content to forget the whole incident had ever happened.

James and the remaining crew stood watching as the bird faded into the distance, its destination a medical facility run by the Bureau. And then, as though it were a cruise no different from any other, each went back to their business, relieved to have the foul cargo gone from their floating home.

WHAT HAD GIVEN Julie the idea to have the picnic on the floor of James' office she would never know, but she realized now that it was exactly what Cassandra needed. The child needed to see that not all men were evil. Cassandra had yet to settle comfortably in her own father's lap and just the sound of a man's voice filled her with terror. The picnic—without the presence of the host—was a good way to introduce the child to one of her rescuers in a slow way. And once she was comfortable with him, perhaps she'd take her to visit some of the other agents—maybe even Steve St. Kitts. Steve had been kind enough to have the office secured so the picnic could take place.

Julie divided the submarine sandwich and set a small portion on Cassandra's paper plate. The child huddled on the floor in the center of the room, her eyes wide and haunted. She had seen James' picture on the wall and all the memories of that day had crashed down upon her in all their violent fury. The diaper was instantly soaked and Julie had helped her change quickly in the private bathroom, grateful that the child's mother had begun providing a diaper bag along with each visit.

"Come eat, Cassandra. This is supposed to be a good picnic and it won't be very good if you go home hungry." She watched the child, shoulders hunched and eyes scanning the walls warily.

"He's not a b-b-b-bad man?" Her blue gaze darted to the security of Julie's friendly face.

"No. Don't you remember? He's the man who broke down the door and covered you with his coat. He covered you, Cassandra. He hid you from the man. He and a bunch of ambulance attendants and other agents and police officers—they all helped you. Wouldn't you like a chance to meet those people and say thank you?"

The girl shrugged her shoulders tighter and scooted closer to Julie, picking up a small piece of the sandwich and forcing a nibble. "He carried me, Miss Julie. He took me out . . ." She whispered the words through her mechanical chewing.

"Yes, he did, and I wish he was here right now to show you that many men are really good people. Only a few are really bad. Your daddy's a good man, isn't he?" Julie bit into her own sandwich and watched the girl nod. They chewed in silence—their food as well as their thoughts.

"Where is he?"

"Special Agent Benedict? He's on a big boat trying to stop another bad man from hurting other people. That's what he does. He stops the bad men and women in the world. Like a lot of other good people do. He does that because Jesus helped him and taught him to help others." Julie watched Cassandra take another bite and scan the walls once more.

"What does that picture say?" She timidly pointed to the needlepoint resting above James' chair and Julie followed the direction of the small finger. A smile came to her mouth and she repeated the words.

"*Revelation 7:17 — For the Lamb at the center of the throne will be their shepherd; he will lead them to springs of living water. And God will wipe away every tear from their eyes.* It's a Bible verse—you know—from the book I've been reading with you. It talks about Jesus. He's called the Lamb of God and this says that someday, when we all get to Heaven, he's going to lead us to a wonderful place and wipe all the tears from our eyes so we'll never be sad again. Just imagine, Cassandra, we'll never hurt or be afraid or cry ever again. Won't that be wonderful?"

The child's eyes grew wide and she nodded eagerly, the first real demonstration of enthusiasm she had displayed. "You mean all these bad feelings in my stomach will go away?"

Julie chuckled. "Yes, Cassandra. Every last one of them. Do you know what dying is?" She watched a shadow drop over the child's face and a small nod accompanied the answer.

"My Granny died last summer. I loved her lots and I miss her. Mommy and Daddy put her in the ground and said that she went to Heaven. Is that how you get to Heaven, Miss Julie? Do you have to go through a cave?"

Round eyes questioned and Julie chuckled again. "Well, if your Granny really loved Jesus, then yes, she is in Heaven. But it doesn't quite work the way you think. When you go to sleep, what happens?"

The child frowned. "I don't know. I can't remember."

"Do you think your body disappears?"

A shake of curls.

"That's right. Your body stays right there, but you don't remember what happens, do you? That's because the real you—the one that thinks and feels—actually lives inside your body and when you go to sleep it stops thinking about all the things you did that day. It's kind of like your body is a sweater that you wear and when it gets old and worn out you take it off. Your Granny's body is the same. Her body—the sweater—is still in the ground, but her spirit—the part that thinks and feels and falls asleep at night and wakes up in the morning—is with Jesus. She can't even feel the pain in her body now because Jesus took her to that wonderful place and wiped away her tears." Julie hoped the child understood. Sometimes it amazed her how brilliant children actually were.

Cassandra chewed another bite of her food in silence, staring hard at the picture, and then she set her sandwich aside and turned to face Julie, her eyes clear and solemn. "I think I'd like to go see Jesus, except that I'd miss Mommy and Daddy. It'll be nice not to hurt or be scared anymore, but I think they need me."

Julie choked and took a quick sip of her juice to cover the swell of emotion. When her throat cleared, she offered an over-bright smile. "I think I would miss you too, dear. As nice as it would be to be with Jesus, I think you should stay here for a few years. Don't you think so?"

The shiny curls bobbled again.

∼∼∼Chapter Twenty-Four

DR. PERRY O'CONNELL stood in the outer corridor drawing in much needed air. He had never seen anything like this before. The five corpses had continued their work of decomposition in spite of the refrigeration provided on ship. It was astounding—and revolting. The stench filtered into the hall and he shook his head, not sure that he wanted to return to the task at hand. But someone had to do it and his staff had abandoned him—all but one assistant with a very strong stomach. How she remained in the forensics lab with that smell was beyond his understanding. Drawing in one final breath of clean air, he turned back to the door that led him to the remains of an unknown assailant's intense wrath.

"IT WAS AN interesting day, to say the least." Steve sounded tired and James wondered if the man ever took a break. "I had Reese check into the background of Agrinoram and he said it was owned by Phelix Corp. This gets more and more interesting as time goes by."

James was weary of having the bulk of his conversations by telephone. It gave him a kink in his neck and he hated the lack of eye contact. "Isn't Phelix Corp. the company being investigated for money laundering? That's been in the news for the last month or so."

"The very same. The problem is this company is owned by an offshore company based in Turks and Caicos—not easily tracked—and Agrinoram is a subsidiary that keeps most of its information off shore with the parent company. We can't get into their records to find out who owns it. Both companies insist that any chemicals made in house are carefully monitored—other than the ones reported stolen five years ago."

"The Beluga whale incident." James felt like a bug caught in a very nasty web.

"So now we're trying to find a way to get the company owners' names and see how they connect to Vietnam—I have no doubt there's a connection somewhere. Incidentally, Reese found some interesting stuff on Sa'ng Phang: loaded offshore bank accounts, pay-offs, email correspondence—that sort of thing. All hidden under secure systems which Reese didn't find too terribly difficult to break through. I don't know what we'd do without him. Too bad the Czar computer didn't pan out . . ." Steve was silent for a moment.

"Dr. O'Connell said this toxin is the worst thing he's ever seen. Imagine this compound in the hands of our enemies? World War III would begin and end in about a week. We really need to find Jeremy Spurgeon."

THE TWO SENIOR citizens eyed Steve with something akin to suspicion. They had gone over this conversation with the authorities so long ago that they couldn't understand why it needed to be brought back to the present.

"I understand you're upset that your son's body has to be exhumed, but we need to make a positive identification to verify that it truly was Jeremy's body—something that wasn't done."

"What? Do you think he's a ghost or something? Or maybe you think he killed somebody and torched our place to hide it? That's foolishness. Jeremy was a good boy. He tried so hard. Such a shame that he didn't have a better start on life." Mrs. Abrams tipped her head to stare at the lines and wrinkles that criss-crossed her aged hands. Thick grey hair was pinned neatly back into a tight bun and framed a narrow, sun-blotched face. At one time in her life she had been a great beauty, and the shadow of that beauty still lingered in the lines of her sagging skin.

Mr. Abrams shook with the slight tremor of the early stages of Parkinson's disease, but his mind was sharp and clear. He nodded his agreement, his few wisps of white hair dancing with the movement. "It broke our hearts to lose the lad. We loved him as our own and still wonder what he would've been had he lived. Surely you don't think he was capable of what you suggest?"

Steve looked at his manicured hands folded neatly and draped over a crossed knee. "I know it's difficult for you—especially after so many years—but this needs to be done." Lifting his gaze, he pinned them with his grim black eyes.

"He or his biological father is linked to every victim and potential victim in our most recent investigation. While I can't give you more than that, I need you to understand that this is a life-and-death matter for a number of people. Forensics will only take a small tissue sample for DNA analysis to compare with a similar sample taken from his father and X-rays of his arms and hands too. And then they will both be buried again immediately. We will treat Jeremy's remains with the utmost respect. I promise." He held them in that disconcerting gaze of his, waiting while they whispered together for a few moments before Mr. Abrams shrugged and nodded in resignation.

"Ok, then. So you have our permission. Is there anything else?"

Steve smiled a brief flicker. "Actually, yes. It would really help if you could give me a full description of the boy. Everything you can think of that will give me a physical, mental and emotional picture of Jeremy. His hair colour, eye colour, habits, accomplishments. Anything."

"My goodness," the old man rumbled in his age worn voice, "you'll be here all day if that's what you want. The boy was a genius. Accomplishments? Where do I begin? Let's see. He was chess champion, got the mathematics award, the science award. The teachers all loved him. They were patient with him because he tried so hard."

Steve frowned and interrupted. "What do you mean, 'patient with him'?"

Mrs. Abrams laid her hand on her husband's arm and inserted herself into the conversation. "Jeremy stuttered terribly. It took ages for him to say just about anything. Some of the kids mocked him or laughed, but the teachers would have none of that. They made certain that he got every opportunity they could give him, hoping that some day he would be able to leave his past abuses behind and become the great man that he had the potential to become. We put him into therapy for almost two years but it didn't make any difference whatsoever. It was almost painful to listen to him speak."

Steve frowned, annoyed that this piece of information had been missing from the files. He would have a chat with Jonas about that. "Do you have a clear photograph of him? Any photos we have are either too young or computer generated and aren't as clear as we'd like. We would have nabbed a school photo, but it seems Jeremy's health deteriorated every time it was class photo day—either that or he was extremely camera shy."

Mrs. Abrams heaved her bulk from the musty armchair and hobbled over to a small curio cabinet, the pain in her swollen ankles evident in her stilted gait. "Yes, he didn't like to have his picture taken. The few we have are candid shots. He didn't know we even had the camera out or he would have disappeared or hidden his face. This is one of the best photos we have of Jeremy. Father here was quite a photographer in his younger days—weren't you, dear?—and we just loved this particular shot." She pulled an eight-by-ten framed portrait from the cabinet and shuffled her way back to the chair where she settled herself again. Holding the photo against her ample bosom, she screwed up her face. "You *are* going to give it back?"

Steve nodded reassuringly and held his hand out. "I'll have one of my agents scan it and return it to you immediately." Dropping his gaze, he studied the picture in silence for a moment, drinking in each detail of the poignant moment frozen for eternity. Jeremy had his arms draped across the shoulders of another boy and a girl. It was quite obvious that the other two were Abrams children as they shared the various features of their parents.

A crooked smile cut across the boy's face and white blond hair ruffled in an unseen breeze. His eyes stared off at some distant scene and the photographer had captured the mischievous glint that lurked in their depths. The other two were draped about him and the laughter shone on their faces as they shared some secret joke. It was a happy time stored for future generations to share. Jeremy's blue eyes showed little of the pain and torment that had plagued him through earlier years and, to the untrained eye, he looked like any other young teen, happy and carefree in a world that was his for the taking. He didn't have the look of a killer. But then—what exactly was the look of a killer like?

Steve frowned and held the photo closer, studying it quietly for a long moment. Pinching the bridge of his nose between thumb and forefinger, he rubbed tired eyes and then lifted his face and offered a final smile. "Thank you so much for your understanding and patience. I'll keep you up to date on what we find."

⚬⚬⚬⚬Chapter Twenty-Five

THEY APPROACHED THE formidable figure who sat next to the seat of power in the small corner of the Bureau. Julie steeled herself for a battle with Sylvia. She didn't think the older woman would disappoint her. "Hi, Sylvia. I'm here to see Special Agent in Charge St. Kitts. I brought a friend."

Sylvia looked over the rims of her glasses and clipped out a command. "Have a seat while I page him." Turning to the small black box on her desk, she pressed a button and waited for a response. "Doctor Holding is here with Cassandra Carpenter to see you."

A disembodied voice drifted quietly through the electronic components. "Oh yes. Thank you Sylvia. Would you please send Dr. Holding in alone for a few moments first? You wouldn't mind keeping an eye on the child for a minute or two?"

Sylvia hesitated and looked as though she had swallowed vinegar. "Yes, sir." And then the intercom was silent and she turned to Julie. "Special Agent in Charge St. Kitts will see you first. The child is to have a seat."

Julie nodded and dropped to her haunches. "Cassandra, I need to talk to Special Agent in Charge St. Kitts for a few minutes. Ms. Lester here will keep an eye on you. You'll be very safe with her, I have no doubt." She flicked a cautious glance at the woman and saw that she had swung back to her computer terminal and continued typing. "I need you to sit on that chair right over there. If you are frightened or you need anything at all, I want you to tell Ms. Lester and she'll come and get me. I'm just in that other room." She pointed to the wall where Sylvia's office ended and Steve's began. "Are you ok with that?" Cassandra nodded cautiously.

Julie returned the nod and walked her to the chair, waiting until the child was comfortably seated with a book open on her lap. She paused for a few moments longer, threw another concerned look at Sylvia's back and opened the door to the office.

"Come in, Doctor. What can I do to help you?" Steve was closing a file folder and pressed the intercom. "Sylvia, hold all my calls while my guests are here." Folding his hands on the desk, he lifted a questioning gaze.

"I was hoping to introduce Cassandra to a man who is good. She needs to see that not all men desire to hurt children."

Steve squirmed in his chair and looked uneasily toward the door. "Ah, I'm not exactly a 'child' type of person. Couldn't you find someone a bit more—child friendly?"

Julie smiled broadly and planted herself in an empty chair. "I did. Look, sir. I know you have to maintain a high level of discipline in order to hold the Agents' trust, but I think you're a lot softer than you let on. All I need is for you to meet her, smile, shake her hand and give her the chance to meet a man without wetting her pants and having a breakdown."

"You're not asking for much, are you?" He lifted the corner of his mouth. "So how do I do this?"

"Just stay seated in the chair, don't move suddenly, don't speak loudly and let her lead the conversation. It might be quiet in here for awhile but she needs to see that she can talk to you and be safe." She rose to open the door, her brows raised in question as she paused for a reply.

"Ok. I'll wait here."

Julie turned the doorknob quietly and pulled the door open a few inches, freezing suddenly at the sight that met her from behind Sylvia's desk. Gesturing quickly, she beckoned for Steve to come see. He moved from behind his desk and peeked over Julie's shoulder to view the picture of Cassandra Carpenter planted on Sylvia's ample lap, thumb in mouth, watching the fast pace of fingers over a keyboard. The woman's arms were folded about the child in a protective embrace, and while the face resumed a stern appearance, there were tears tracking down aging cheeks. Slowly, they closed the door again and then made conversation loud enough to announce their entrance. Without turning to face them, the older secretary set the child on the ground and turned back to her typing, the keys snapping with the rapid movement of tense fingers.

"I'D LIKE TO know how you managed to miss something as important as Jeremy's foster parents. We have all the links, and you—our resident computer genius—have missed two important leads—something you've never done before." Steve's eyes crackled with anger as he leaned over his desk, fingers steepled and braced to hold his weight.

"Look, sir. I told you that the Czar's computer virus backtracked and fried my computer. It was part of the initial code—you know—enter a computer as a harmless file, expand into a nasty file and completely fry everything. I thought I had all the right firewalls up. We're dealing with a ruddy genius here and he got the better of me. I'm sorry, sir. Look, if you want to check my computer, go ahead. It's toast and I couldn't stop it."

Reese watched his boss hover over the desk and he felt the sweat trickling down the back of his neck. Furious at himself for his own stupidity and laziness, Reese hoped that he could talk himself out of this corner. For too long, he'd been the prima donna of the technology wing. He'd been careless. Of course Steve would put another agent on the Czar computer, and he had been too cocky to see it coming. The Bureau Chief would never let a lead go that easily when he so badly needed its information. Forcing himself to keep calm, Reese blew out a breath and reached for the inner pocket of his jacket, extracting the small leather folder that held his FBI badge. "Do you want my badge, sir? If you don't trust me, then maybe I shouldn't be here." Extending the small symbol of power, he waited and watched his boss's face.

Steve straightened, holding Reese's gaze for a moment longer, and then folded himself into his chair. "Keep the badge, Reese. I'm just getting a bit frustrated with this whole thing. Every time I get somewhere, I find myself

backing up ten paces. I'll let it go if you will. Send your
computer down to Jonas so he can see what he can do. I
guess it was an easy enough mistake to skip over Jeremy's
past. But Reese, we can't afford these kinds of mistakes.
Keep sharp, will you?" Reese nodded and left the office.

JONAS STUMBLED over the threshold of the dark bar. The
smell of smoke, sweat and perfume hung in the air and he
coughed. If it hadn't been a favourite spot for many of the
Bureau's agents, the dive would probably have gone under
long ago. It had that tough, cowboy charm to it that seemed
to coincide with some of the agent's baser emotions. He
only went there when work backed him into a corner. And
it had.

A buxom waitress greeted him at the door, her middle-
aged skin hidden under layers of heavy makeup.

"What can I get you, darlin'? You want a booth or a
table?"

"A booth." He mumbled his reply. Jonas didn't want
company. He had a lot to think about. The things he was
finding in his research didn't sit well with him. Sitting down
in a corner booth, he slid as far into the corner as he could.
"I'll have whisky."

The waitress raised an eyebrow and scanned his tidy
suit and carefully coifed hair. He didn't look like a whiskey
kind of guy. He often got that reaction.

"Can I get you a menu?" He shook his head. The waitress quickly wiped the table with her damp cloth and gave
him a smirk before heading to the bar.

"Well, look who dragged his scrawny carcass in here?" A voice bellowed from across the room and Jonas cringed as Reese pulled himself to his feet and staggered his way through the crowded dance floor. "You got some nerve showing up here, Taylor. You try to take my job and then you show up to rub my face in it?"

Some of the patrons looked up from their drinks and the hum of conversation died. Jonas shifted his eyes around the room and swallowed. He wouldn't dare take on Reese on his own. Hopefully there were enough agents in the room to keep the man's belligerence at bay.

"Reese, I'm not trying to take your job. I'm just following orders. I haven't really found much, anyway."

"Liar!" Reese swayed and a few chairs in the room shifted. "You just don't think the old guy can keep up. Well, I'll show you how good I am at my job."

"Look, Reese. I don't want your job. And I don't think you're too old." Jonas stood, his hands spread wide. "Why don't I just leave and you can enjoy your evening here."

Reese planted a meaty palm on Jonas' shoulder and shoved. "So you're a coward too, huh? Can't stand and fight? You can stab me in the back but you can't face me?"

A hand gripped Reese's arm and he swung around to face another agent who had stood up to join them.

"Hey, man. You've had a little bit too much. Why don't I take you home?"

Reese glared at the agent and snorted, pulling his arm away. "I don't want to stay anyway."

The two of them left the bar and Jonas hunched down into his booth. A few minutes later the whisky arrived and he sipped it slowly. It wouldn't do for him to get out of control. He'd need his wits about him in the days ahead. Reese hadn't just missed Jeremy's background. Someone had sent a virus *from* a computer in the Bureau. The fur would really hit the fan when Steve found out that Reese missed that one too. Jonas didn't really want to be around for that.

Tossing the drink back, he finished it, slapped a bill on the table and rose to leave. The room was still quiet and he realized that several pairs of eyes rested on him. He wouldn't be coming back to this bar for awhile.

~~~Chapter Twenty-Six

T HINGS WEREN'T GOING at all the way he wanted them to. Slipping into his cubicle, he scanned the room carefully and pulled a disk from his coat pocket, loaded it into the hard drive and hit download. While the deadly program mangled his computer, he casually scanned the room, keeping an eye out for unwanted visitors. It would be difficult to explain the destruction of a Bureau computer. When the quiet whirring and chewing had finished, he removed the disk, slipped it in his pocket and then scooped up any evidence of his presence. Slipping out into the hall, he headed to the elevator, nodding to a passing agent as he punched the down button. A smirk twitched the corner of his mouth. Anyone trying to open that computer would have a fun time trying it. They'd never be able to retrieve anything off of that machine. If the disk had done its job, they'd have all the proof needed that the Czar computer virus had come into the Bureau instead of the other way around.

"JAMES, WE'RE bringing the ship back to dock. Mr. Harridan has decided to reimburse all the passengers anyway, so it's not going to make much difference, and that way, I can get a team on board to scour the ship from stem to stern. The Captain will keep the crew on board—just in case Phang wasn't alone—and as long as no more passengers come down with our little illness, you'll be on shore by tomorrow afternoon."

James could feel himself relax at the good news. This was supposed to have been a vacation, but it had ended up feeling more like prison. "Does Julie know?"

"No," Steve coughed out a dry chuckle, "but I won't keep you long, so you can tell her. I'll have Reese meet you at the dock. I'm sure you two will want to compare notes. He's not very happy with me right now."

"Oh?" James plugged an ear against the merry tunes in the theatre behind him.

"I chewed him out a bit. He was in charge of the research for all the victims and he completely missed the link between Jeremy Spurgeon and the LeBlancs. An oversight—maybe—but that and the screw up with the Czar computer makes me wonder if he's getting too old for the job."

"I'll talk to him when I see him. Maybe he's having marital problems again. That tends to rattle him through and through. Rita has put up with a lot over the years and she tends to rebel on occasion." Pulling at the tight collar of his tux, James tossed a glance at the Broadway show through the glass doors of the theatre. Shrugging, he turned his back and began walking toward the promenade deck doors. "Steve, is there something you're not telling me? I can hear that note that you get in your voice when you have a suspicion."

Silence greeted the question. "Steve?"

"James, Jonas thinks that there may be someone working from inside the Bureau. Even if it isn't Reese—and I'm not saying it is—no one had access to the Czar computer. We've viewed the security tapes a dozen times from all angles and no one was near it. The tampering came through the internet, and as soon as we found out about the lottery, we tapped into their web connections. I can't imagine there being a computer out there with enough viral power to squeeze through any one of the dozens of firewalls and anti-virus programs Reese has designed and installed in his computer, but he tells me that there was a program installed in the Czar computer and, when he tried to tap into it, the thing tracked back into his computer and destroyed every component it touched. I had him drop his hard drive off with Jonas under the pretense that Jonas would try to figure out what kind of virus it was. The truth is that I've asked Jonas to retrieve and copy as many files and programs as he can. It just doesn't feel right that Reese missed this."

"Oh, come on, sir!" A couple who had been leaning against the rail a dozen feet away turned to peer at James through the night sky, and he turned and walked down the deck out of hearing range, his tux jacket flapping in the night wind. "You can't honestly believe that Reese has gone bad. He's been with the Bureau since . . ."

"Since he resigned from the military after Vietnam." Steve spoke it quietly but James heard it like a shout.

"So you do think he's turned?" It hurt to voice it and James swallowed against the knot in his throat. They'd been partners for . . . well . . . forever. Reese had saved his life on more than one occasion and James had returned the favour just as many times. This was too much to swallow. "So why are you sending him to pick me up?" Silence again. "Oh, I get it. You want me to go fishing—see if I can get him to say something that will bury him. That's not fair, sir. I can't do it." Again nothing. James sighed. It was time to end this job. But not yet. "I'll do what I can." Steve had said nothing to make him change his mind. Steve seldom had to.

The lead settled into his gut as he flipped the phone shut. Reese, a traitor. Unbelievable. But he had been to Vietnam. James gripped the phone, looking far out into the murky water. The urge to pitch the thing into the drink was overwhelming, but it wouldn't change what Steve suspected. Reese, a betrayer. Suddenly he didn't look forward to his phone call with Julie. This was one little tidbit he knew he couldn't tell her. He'd keep it short and call her back in the morning. She'd understand.

~~~Chapter Twenty-Seven

"I THINK I WILL try hard to forgive you." Julie's voice carried a light reprimand. "Only because I know you did it out of concern. So what becomes of your tennis matches?"

"I'll find a new partner. Dex crossed a line there. I don't just stand aside with something like that. I'm glad you understand, Julie. I couldn't just sit here and do nothing." As much as she had tried to sound annoyed, James knew that Julie understood his need to protect her. And Dexter *had* crossed boundaries he shouldn't have. Maybe Reese went a bit overboard, but the point was well made. He'd call Dex when he got back and they'd have a real heart-to-heart. They weren't exactly best buddies, but the relationship did go back a long ways. "So is there anything new going on since we last chatted?"

"As a matter of fact—yes. While we were waiting for our little meeting with Special Agent in Charge St. Kitts, Cassandra introduced herself to Sylvia with a most interesting question. She asked her if she was a Christian."

James stopped in mid-chew and almost choked on the mouthful of scrambled eggs. "You're joking? And what was Ms. Crusty's response to that?"

"James. That's not nice." Julie reprimanded him softly.

"I know. I'm sorry. It's one of those spiritual battles I'm still fighting. So what happened?" He sunk his teeth into a jam-slathered piece of toast, leaving Julie to carry the conversation for the next few moments. She didn't disappoint him.

"It was interesting, to say the least. I left her with Sylvia while I popped into Steve's office to see if he had a few moments. I had already warned him earlier that I might be bringing Cassandra to meet him, but I figured it might take weeks for her to agree to it. He cleared his schedule right away. Sometimes Steve really surprises me. He comes across as gruff and unemotional and then he pushes aside an overloaded agenda for the sake of a six-year-old. I think he's a softy deep down. I told him that. Not sure he was impressed with my assessment but he got over it quickly." James grunted. "Anyway, I was in there longer than I had planned. He wanted to know what to say and what not to say, so I gave him a few pointers. When we went back out to the waiting area, there was Cassandra, plopped down on Sylvia's lap. The woman looked like she was going to bawl. Soon as she knew we were there she set Cassandra onto the floor and went back to her typing like nothing had happened. There's more to Sylvia than we know. We didn't want to embarrass her, so we acted as though we hadn't seen anything."

"Sylvia? Tears? I didn't think the two words went together. Ok, so maybe I was wrong about her, but you have to admit she is pretty prickly. And she does go out of her way to make life difficult." James wiped his mouth with a serviette and frowned at the blob of jam on his T-shirt.

"Yes, well, Cassandra is a bit too young to understand the meaning of discretion. You know how sometimes people find it easier to talk to children or strangers? Well, Sylvia's obviously one of them. When I went in to talk to Steve, Cassandra got frightened and asked if she could see me. Sylvia pulled her up onto her lap and asked if she'd like to try typing. Cassandra was quite thrilled about playing on a "'puter." That's when she asked the dreaded question. James, she told me all about it. Never in a million years did I expect her to move from silence into full conversation so quickly. It's nothing short of a miracle. She said that Sylvia got all sad and told her that Christians weren't always what they seemed. James, Cassy defended me and said I was a good person and that if I said Jesus was real and kind then he just had to be." Julie's voice caught. "What an awesome responsibility we have as Christians."

"So what did Sylvia say to that?" He placed a fist over his mouth and belched quietly away from the phone.

"It's sad, James. Cassandra said that Sylvia's dad was a preacher, but not like the kind you and I are familiar with. He felt it was his godly duty to teach his daughter how to be a good wife, and after he got her pregnant, he turned on her and accused her before the church of being a loose woman. He kicked her out of her home at seventeen years old. When she lost the baby, she just figured that if there was a God, he hated her."

James could hear Julie's pain and he blew out a loud sigh. "Sylvia told her all this? Why would an adult reveal something so personal?" He could almost hear the shrug.

"Who knows? It happens though. Sometimes people bottle it up so tightly that the most innocent thing pops the cork and it all boils out. I don't think Cassandra understood everything, but she seemed to know that Sylvia was hurting. And I would imagine Sylvia's feeling pretty foolish this morning. Poor Steve. He'll have an extra dose of crustiness to deal with today."

"So what did our little Cassie say to it all?"

"Oh, James. I wanted to cry. She got that big-eyed, grown up look on her face and said that she told her about the needlepoint verse on your wall and how Jesus would someday wipe away her tears. And then we showed up and Sylvia shut down."

James rolled the paper napkin into a ball and stuffed it in his empty glass before pushing the tray aside. "Out of the mouths of babes, hey? Is this world so full of sick people that a guy would do that to his own daughter? I guess I owe Sylvia an apology for my attitude."

"Yah. Except she doesn't know we know. I think I'm just going to try to be a bit nicer to her and let God do the work. She might just start to believe what Cassandra told her."

"Point taken. I'll do the same when I get home. Which brings me to what I was too tired to tell you about last night. Reese is picking me up at the dock this afternoon. They're bringing the ship back. The passengers aren't impressed but they'll get over it when they find out that Sandy has reimbursed them completely. So how did your evening with him go? Was he a gentleman? Did he behave himself? Did he make a pass? Try to impress you and schmooze you into liking him more than me?"

Julie laughed. "Yes, yes and yes. Remind me never to say yes to a night at the opera again. He was quite a gentleman and I think he did rather regret that you and I are an item—I made that quite plain simply by talking about how wonderful you are. You'll be happy to know we shook hands and declared ourselves friends. He wished us well and didn't try to ask for another evening out. Says he approves of the match."

"And?"

"And I found out all sorts of naughty things about the man I love. Remind me to share them with you when you get back on land. It was nice meeting him after hearing about him for the past eight months."

"Has it been that long? I think it's time this relationship moved into high gear then, don't you? Maybe he'll loan us the honeymoon suite on one of his floating hotels." James rested his forehead against his hand. His voice had dropped into soft low tones.

"Now why would he need to do that?" The laughter disappeared.

"Because I think we're going to need it soon."

"You don't say?"

"Yes—I do."

~~~Chapter Twenty-Eight

"SIR, I'VE CONTACTED the airport. There's a flight if you want me to hold it for you. Can I book it, or would you rather wait?"

Her voice crackled through the speaker phone and the man sat like a granite statue for a moment before replying. And then, as though freed from his unseen restraints, he swivelled his torn and rusted chair around and leaned toward the phone. "Go ahead and book it, Doris. I said I'd make it for the convention and I don't want to disappoint the powers that be, do I? Once you've done that, take the next few days off. I won't be here to keep you running about, anyway."

He could hear the hesitation in her voice. He wasn't himself and this efficient secretary could pick up deviations easily. If he continued to step out of his normal patterns, he would certainly begin to draw attention to himself. But there was nothing else to be done. Whatever trail he'd left behind had been obscured. Anyone who knew of his father and his connections to Vietnam was dead. But it wouldn't hurt to be out of the country just in case.

The man rose from his creaking chair and walked to the small safe that held his most precious possessions. A few spins of the dial and the door swung open with effort. There they sat. The medals. They gleamed their various metallic tones from their nest in the shoe box and he felt a surge of pride at what they signified. No matter what the military had done, no matter how foul some of their schemes had been, he would always know that his father had died fighting and he, the son, could do no less. He would fight to make right the wrongs forced upon him and his family . . . as his father would have done had he lived long enough to do so.

REESE PARKED A hip against Jonas' desk and sat there for a few moments. Jonas abandoned the file he had been working on and looked up at the large man, uncertain as to what kind of greeting he would receive. Reese remained still, pinching the bridge of his nose between his thumb and forefinger. Opening his eyes, he looked at Jonas through narrow slits—as though the daylight hurt.

"Look, Jonas. About last night . . ."

"Don't worry about it, Reese." Jonas looked down at his desk. He didn't want eye contact. He didn't want any kind of interaction, if the truth were known.

"No. I need to tell you I'm sorry. I got out of line. Too much to drink." Reese looked across the busy room, the muscles in his jaw twitching. "When you get to be my age, it isn't a big leap to start imagining that the powers that be see you as an old horse ready for pasture. Who knows? Maybe I am too old for this job. I missed too much on this. Instead of insulting you, I should have been thanking you. My screw-ups could have caused some serious problems for my partner." He brought his focus back to the red hair in front of him. "Can we just forget it happened?" He offered a hand. "Friends?"

Jonas looked at the outstretched hand. He wanted to reject it. He wanted to get up and walk out, but that wasn't a good idea. Reaching up, he took the hand, gave it a shake and withdrew. "Just so long as you know that I wasn't trying to kick you out, Reese. We work together here. At least that's how I was trained. I'm supposed to watch your back and you're supposed to watch mine."

Reese stood then and let out a sigh of relief. Clapping Jonas on the back, he turned to leave. "So long as there's no hard feelings, right?"

Jonas looked at him. "Yah. Yah, right." Reese turned and left the room.

JULIE GENTLY HELD onto Cassandra's hand as they wandered through the halls of the Bureau—through areas that a child was permitted to see. They had decided to visit the crowded office of the lower ranked agents. She was grateful that Cassie's parents had agreed to the daily sessions. It had made the child's improvement take place just that much more quickly—with divine intervention to nudge it along, of course.

They chatted amiably, but Julie saw that Cassandra continued to regard the smiles of the male agents warily; she grew silent when they spoke and dropped her gaze to the floor if they came too close. And yet, the child had done incredibly well with Steve St Kitts. Julie smiled as her mind went back to the meeting of the day before. Steve had done well too. What a lark! The man professed to be uncomfortable around children and yet, the moment Cassandra entered the room he visibly changed. Light danced about the depths of his eyes and the chocolate-hued skin of his face crinkled into a small smile.

Cassandra shadowed Julie and slipped quietly onto her lap, facing away from the desk, and Julie deliberately turned her body around to force the young girl into facing Steve. Then she spoke gently, Saying, "Cassandra, I'd like you to meet Special Agent in Charge Steve St. Kitts. To make it easier, you may call him Mr. St. Kitts." The child said nothing and pulled herself tighter against Julie's chest. Silence filled the room, interrupted by the occasional rustle of clothing as one or the other of the adults shifted in their chairs. Julie made eye contact with Steve and shrugged apologetically. He waited.

When no one spoke, curiosity finally overcame the girl's fear and she took a quick glance at the man behind the desk. Julie didn't know or understand what went through the little girl's mind, but a sudden clenching of the jaw and steely determination in the eyes indicated a shift in the mind of the victim. Slowly, she slid from Julie's lap, her gaze never leaving Steve's calm face, and walked around behind his desk and stiffly took his hand. Steve's smile broadened as he gently scooped her onto his knee and sat still, holding her only with his soft eyes.

Julie smiled a broader smile as the mental image lingered and she squeezed the small hand grasped firmly in her own. "Would you like to meet Special Agent Benedict's partner? He's another man who tries to stop bad people."

Cassandra lifted worried and hesitant eyes to her guardian. "I g-g-g-g-guess so."

Weaving through the crowded office, the two headed for a cluttered desk and a man hunched over a stack of papers. "Hey, Reese. How's it going?" Julie eyed the empty space strangely nestled into the clutter. "Where's your computer?"

"Jonas has it. It got fried. He's going to see what he can find." Reese swung back in his chair and looked down his nose at the small figure clinging to Julie's side. "And who have we here? Don't I know you?" He squinted as recent memories of the rescue surfaced. "You're Cassandra, aren't you?" She nodded and stepped back. Without waiting for the answer, the older agent turned his attention to Julie. "So your boyfriend is coming back today. Want to accompany me to the dock to retrieve our wayward sailor?"

His eyes twinkled and Julie laughed. "I have the next hour with Cassandra and then her parents will be here. Sorry, I've got to pass. Oh, and by the way, Reese, as much as I don't like strong arm tactics, thanks for getting Dex to back off."

Reese stood and pulled his rumpled suit jacket from off the back of his chair. "You're more than welcome. Never did like lawyers. They always seem to let the wrong people go free. You sure you don't want to hitch a ride with me? I'll even turn my back when the two of you get all mushy." He made a show of closing his eyes and kissing the air. Opening his eyes again, he winked at Cassandra and she giggled, causing Julie to look at her in surprise. "Disembarkation begins in . . ." he threw a look at his watch ". . . five minutes. While I'm working my way through the snarl of traffic, he'll have time to get his bags and be ready. It shouldn't take an hour. I just thought it'd be fun to give him a grand reception. What do you say?"

Julie looked from Reese's questioning face to the shy child beside her. No. It wouldn't be right to take the child out of the building. Besides the extra emotional strain it might cause, she hadn't received that kind of parental permission. "Sorry, Reese. I can't. But we'll be here when the two of you get back."

"Your loss." He winked again and headed for the door, holding it open for Julie and Cassandra to pass through.

"At least we can walk you to the lobby. Can't we?" She looked down at her companion and smiled at the small nod. Cassandra stared at the floor.

Placing herself between Reese and the child, Julie took her hand and proceeded to chat amiably with James' partner as they clicked down the hollow halls to the warm room at the building's entrance. Just as Reese would have exited the building, a muffled ring interrupted the light banter. Julie stopped, clicked open her purse and rifled into its depths, finally pulling out her cell phone. "Dr. Holding here . . . Oh, hello, Mrs. Carpenter. Yes, Cassandra has had a productive session." She looked down at the child, who had wandered to a chair nestled into the corner of the lobby. "I see. I didn't think you were leaving until tomorrow. Well, that's wonderful! May I tell Cassandra? I'm sure she'll be thrilled."

Reese looked on, curiosity holding him. Julie went to Cassandra and squatted down in front of the child. "Cassandra, that was your mom on the phone." Blue eyes looked up from their study of the paisley patterned carpet. "Remember that trip to Disney you were supposed to go on tomorrow?" A nod answered and a rare show of excitement flickered in the azure depths. "Guess what? You get to go today! Your mom said they were able to bump up the flight. They'll be here to get you in ten minutes. Isn't that exciting?" Cassandra nodded and grabbed Julie's hand, offering a gap-toothed grin.

"So I guess it's just going to be the two of us meeting James, then?" Reese parked himself in an overstuffed couch tucked behind a steel and glass coffee table.

"I can't expect you to wait for me. You go on ahead. I'll still be here when James comes back." Julie looked up from her perch in front of her patient.

"Don't be silly. What's a few minutes here or there? I can wait. And James will thank me." He smiled encouragingly and made a funny face at Cassandra. The child giggled again. After a moment, her gaze dropped once more to the busy pattern of the rug. Reese shrugged and lifted his eyebrows, waiting for Julie's answer.

She shifted her thoughts back to the child and glanced at the phone still in her hand. Tucking it into her pocket, Julie pulled herself to her feet and moved to the chair beside Cassandra. "Well . . . if you insist." Her lips widened into a bright smile. It would be a nice surprise to be at the dock waiting for James.

"I insist." Reese stretched sideways to the small end table and pulled a *Time* magazine off the shiny surface. Snapping the glossy paper open, he turned his attention away from Julie as though to prevent any further argument, and she grinned and focused her full attention on Cassandra in the remaining moments before the Carpenters arrived to retrieve her.

~~~~Chapter Twenty-Nine

"**S**O WHERE IS Reese now?" Steve had picked up his jacket off the edge of the chair and was slipping into it as quickly as possible. The small stack of files on his desk were scooped up and unceremoniously chuffed into the open safe. With a flick of the wrist, the safe door swung shut and he spun the dial and scanned the room for any other stray documents that should be secured before he left.

"I don't know, sir. The last time I saw him, he was with Dr. Holding and the little girl she's been working with." In spite of the coolly efficient look Jonas aimed for, he usually only succeeded in appearing flustered. And, at the moment, very worried.

"So tell me again. Tell me everything." Steve pushed past the FBI computer technician and pulled his office door open. "Sylvia, see if you can raise Reese for me. Tell him that he needs to return to the office—lie to him—I don't care—tell him I've got a lead on the toxin—or better yet, that we may have another victim and we need him back here to do a background search. Do whatever it takes, but don't make it sound desperate. I don't need him panicking. He might have Dr. Holding and the Carpenter child with him."

Sylvia threw a confused look at her boss and scrambled to pick up the phone.

With an impatient gesture, he indicated for Jonas to follow and Steve stalked off down the hall toward the lobby where Julie, Cassandra and Reese had last been seen.

Jonas scooped up his own stack of papers and scrambled to catch his boss, talking a mile a minute as they walked. "Well, sir. Like I said, I didn't see how Reese couldn't get into the Czar computer. I had no problem with it at first. And then all of a sudden it wasn't accessible and I thought that was strange—especially since the Bureau had already set up security systems around it—systems that I still had access to. No one outside the Bureau would have been able to get anywhere near that system, so I knew it had to be a firewall from somewhere here in the Bureau.

"Reese had already said the Czar's virus program destroyed his computer. But it hadn't—because at the time there wasn't a virus there. And he got careless, thinking no one else was in the system. I checked some of the other agents' files and Reese sent them emails and files a couple of minutes after he allegedly lost his computer—some last-minute stuff, by the looks of it. Stuff he probably didn't want to have to enter into the system again. He likely figured no one would put it together. I probably wouldn't have either, if Ken hadn't showed me a stupid email joke that Reese passed on to him, dated three minutes after his system was documented as having shut down. He got a bit careless there. So I hacked into his computer while I could and—well—you already know what I found." Jonas was panting, trying to keep up with Steve's long strides.

"So tell me again. I need to hear it again."

"Yes, sir." Jonas shuffled through the bundle of loose papers, struggling to keep them in a firm grip as he pounded along the hall. "I found files on the Vietnam War—and some guy called Nam. There were a bunch of documents pulled out of staff files from . . . let me see . . ." he pulled out a page, "from the same year Robert Spurgeon took a bullet and lost his leg. And then . . ."

Again the shuffle and out came another couple of sheets stapled together. Jonas held them out as though Steve could see the words. "I found the stuff you wanted on Jeremy Spurgeon—his adoption stuff—everything—except it has been tampered with. He was trying to erase all links to Jeremy—trying to make Jeremy disappear.

"Sir, if you hadn't put me onto Victor LeBlanc's file when you did, I would have never found the link with Jeremy. Again, Reese got careless and kept a copy of the files—sort of. You can never really delete anything from a computer unless you take a magnet to it and even then . . . I went into the hard drive and found the ghost files and emails. I'd already gone to Children's Services and found Jeremy, but then the next day he was gone. So when you gave me Reese's computer, I went right into those ghost files and there he was."

Jonas began to hand the document to Steve, realized he wasn't interested and gave up sorting through his files. "I found references to Sa'ng Phang and one email from a hotmail account that talked about the 'strategy behind the vengeance.' It was signed SP and made a reference to 'the General' and 'the nurse' in not-so-friendly terms."

Another shuffling of papers followed. "I also found all kinds of chemical info. It lists the ingredients for Agent Orange. He went through his own account. Personally, I would have used a hotmail under a false name, but it was like he didn't think he'd get caught." Steve threw Jonas a look and he blushed. "Reese got careless. That's the bottom line. His loss, our gain. There's a tentative mention of Phelix Corp. but nothing that incriminates them—and nothing that tells us who owns them. Did you find that out, by the way?" Jonas turned his bottle caps to his chief, only to receive a sharp reprimand.

"Focus, Jonas!"

"Sorry, sir." He dropped his eyes back to the top sheet on his small stack. "There is enough there to link Phang to the murders and convict Reese with tampering with a lottery and aiding in murder. But I have nothing on the few references to this guy named Nam. Do you think it could be Jeremy?" A grunt was the only reply. "I also found all the doctored files that made it look like Phang was in this alone. Whoever is at the helm of this has sure got his back covered well.

"I—er—ah—borrowed the files and have them all stored on a disk in my desk drawer. If Reese knew I got into his computer while it still worked he'd be hopping mad. When I finally got his computer, it was totally fried. I have no doubt it was a disk download. He's probably made his own destruction virus. If I hadn't made a classified file search and destroy program of my own a few years ago, I might not have recognized the symptoms."

Steve stopped and stared at him. "Why on earth would you want a file search and destroy program in your computer?"

Jonas returned the look as though it was the craziest question Steve could ever have asked. "Well . . . to protect my files, of course. Anyone trying to hack into my computer would trigger a dissolve function and all my files would go up in smoke—and so would theirs. And then the police would show up at their door because I have the whole thing linked to GPS tracking." Steve's shocked expression prodded him to continue. "Oh, don't worry, sir. I back up all my files onto a USB stick every time I use them. I can reload the files into any computer I want. That's how I know Reese wasn't aware of my presence. He probably would have struck back and then his hard drive really would have been baked."

"Jonas!" Steve shook his head incredulously. "Do you realize what you're saying?" He resumed his brisk walk while Jonas scrambled to catch up.

"Oh. I see what you mean sir. Yes. That wouldn't have been good in this case, I guess. Good thing Reese *didn't* hack in. We would have lost everything. I'll have to rethink that, sir. So anyway, I dug through what was left of his computer and there's no doubt—Reese sure downloaded the mother of all viruses. It completely smoked his computer. There's really nothing left worth sorting through."

Steve entered the lobby with Jonas huffing behind him and stopped short at the sight of Mr. and Mrs. Carpenter pulling a light sweater onto their young daughter.

Taking a deep breath, he calmed himself and turned to the agent. "Stay here, Jonas. I need to talk to Cassandra and

I don't want you frightening her." Slowly, he approached, his broad smile not quite reaching his eyes. "Good day, Miss Carpenter." He dropped to his haunches and allowed her a few feet of space.

"Cassandra, I need to ask you some questions. Will you speak to me?" Not waiting for an answer, Steve kept his voice calm. "Cassandra, where's Dr. Holding?"

Cassandra plucked at her pants and kept her eyes pinned to the shiny tips of Steve's leather shoes. Her mouth worked hard to form each consonant and he cringed at the painful process.

"She went with the man—Mr. Reese. They went to get Mr. James from the boat." And then she turned and planted her face in her mother's skirt.

Steve dropped his head for a brief second. If Sylvia couldn't get him to return to the Bureau . . .

Pulling himself to his feet, he took several strides away from the small cluster of people, stopping as he faced an empty hallway. Scooping his phone from his jacket pocket, he punched in his secretary's line and dropped his voice to hushed tones. "Sylvia, did you get a response from Reese?"

"No, sir. He's not answering." Her harsh tones could be heard beyond the small phone's ear piece.

"Get me Dr. Holding's cell phone number immediately. I'm going to try Reese's number myself. Call me back in about a minute." Covering the phone, he turned to Jonas. "Grab a car and get your tail down to the cruise ship docks to pick up James. If you see Reese, just act casual until some back-up arrives. We don't need Julie paying the price for rash action." He punched in Reese's cell phone number, hoping that the agent was simply away from his phone. No answer. Shaking his head, he covered the mouthpiece with a hand and whispered. "This isn't good. Reese isn't picking up and he always answers his phone. Are you sure he doesn't know you hacked his computer?"

Jonas shrugged, "I guess it's possible that he does."

Hitting the end button, Steve immediately dialed the number Sylvia had passed on to him. If that's the case . . ." he stopped as Julie's phone rang.

"If that's the case," Jonas interjected, "Dr. Holding's in trouble."

∼∼Chapter Thirty

THE SHRILL TONES of Julie's phone interrupted her conversation once again and she reached into her coat pocket and pulled the instrument from it. "This thing can be such a nuisance. Can you hold on a second while I get this?" Reese nodded and concentrated on his driving as he wove in and out of the busy San Diego traffic. Julie hit the talk button and pressed the phone to her ear. "Dr. Holding here."

Steve's voice came to her in a soft whisper. "Julie, don't change your facial features and try not to react any differently than if I were a client. Understand?"

Julie smiled and shifted into a light tone. "Oh, hello, Kathy. How are you? It's been awhile."

"Very good. You're with Reese aren't you?"

"Yes, Kathy. I am still working as a psychologist."

"As soon as you get to the dock, I want you to leave Reese and head right to James. Reese is involved in the cruise ship murders. I can't tell you more right now, but you need to get to safety without alerting him. I'll call James and let him know what's up. Understood?"

"Certainly, Kathy. Look, I can't talk right now. I'm actually on my way to pick up a friend. Why don't I call you back when I get home, ok? Talk to you soon." Julie flipped the phone shut and slipped it into her coat pocket.

A deep sigh escaped from Reese and Julie threw him a sidelong glance. And then he spoke. "You're not a very good actress, Julie." His voice had changed—softened—grown serious. It was a voice she hadn't heard before.

"I don't know what you mean." She threw a look of innocence at him and then cringed when he laughed at her effort.

"Julie, I could tell the caller was a man. I could hear a male voice—quietly, but I could hear it. Steve?"

Julie grew silent and quickly turned away, forcing her suddenly stiff gaze out the passenger window to avoid showing that he'd hit the mark. She let silence answer for her.

"What? Did he tell you I'm involved with the cruise ship killings?" She threw a surprised look at him and he laughed again. "I thought maybe they knew. Jonas is really good with the computer. I should have been paying a bit more attention. Steve kind of gave it away when he gave me that lecture about missing too many leads. He'd have been better to have said nothing. Too bad it had to happen now. I was hoping I could bluff my way through and move on with my life, but . . . I guess I can't really go pick up James now, can I? I'm not really sure what to do with you, though. I didn't intend to get you involved." He turned and looked hard at her, clearly unable to come up with a solution. When Julie refused to return the look, he sighed again and focused on driving.

"So are you going to kill me like you did all those innocent people?" Her teeth were clenched and her eyes angry.

"Innocent?" Reese snorted. "Hardly innocent. And if you want to get technical, I haven't really killed anybody. So maybe I helped with the planning. But I didn't kill them." He leaned back into his seat and flipped the right hand signal. The vehicle veered around the corner and he began a series of turns and twists that led away from the ship docks and into a seedier part of the city.

"Did you know that the Vietnam War was the genesis of some of the cruellest weapons next to the A-bomb? No?" He tossed a dead look her way. "Yep. Our fearless leaders concocted a nasty batch of chemicals, ignored all warnings to use caution, multiplied the doses exponentially and sprayed right over top their own men. I should know. I commanded a unit that had to traipse through the jungles after they had been decimated. I was stuck with the clean up duty—of sorts. You know, follow along after each battle and pick up the pieces of our guys, sifting through the enemy's bodies just in case one was alive. That kind of thing. I saw the devastation—watched the innocent die with the guilty. Enough of my guys have had to pay the price too. That stuff they sprayed doesn't just disappear. It soaks into the plants and the soil. You walk through it. It brushes against you. Soaks into your clothes, your skin. I'm one of the lucky ones who hasn't gotten sick from it—yet. I figure it's just a matter of time, though."

He took another sharp right and the car dipped down onto a slanted driveway that led to an underground garage. The silence was interrupted by the scraping of the tail pipe against pock marked pavement as the car bottomed out.

And then Reese spoke again, as though he had gone back in time and was reliving the things he had seen. "Vietnamese and American alike got dosed. And they died in very nasty ways." His jaw clenched and then he returned to the present and turned a hard look on Julie. "No, my dear Dr. Holding. Those people who died on board ship were far from innocent. They just got a taste of their own medicine."

Julie nodded in a placating way, trying hard to concentrate on his words while she shifted inch by inch in her seat. She could feel the bulge of her cell phone in the pocket of her coat where she had dumped it after talking to Steve. But the weight of it had pulled that portion of her coat down between the seat and the door. She would have to pull it out before she could ever reach her phone. And she would have to keep Reese busy with his own emotions in order to do it. "You must be pretty angry at a lot of people, then."

"You have no idea." He wound his way through the dark halls of the underground garage, peering into the darkness. Leaning forward, he flipped on the headlights and continued to direct the car further back into the empty cavern.

"Do you really think that by getting even you'll feel better?" The cloth of her coat was bunched tightly in her hand and she walked her fingers down until she found the slit of her pocket. *Just a few more seconds.* Her right hand slipped carefully into her coat pocket and she gripped her phone. As though blind, she groped slowly, touching the buttons one by one until she found the one she needed. Bottom left corner. Recall. Hitting it twice, she relaxed as the small cell phone automatically dialed the last call received—Steve's cell phone. She likely wouldn't hear a reply, but hopefully, if she called enough times, he'd figure it out. If he did, they would be able to get a satellite lock on her.

"Probably not, but I'll have the satisfaction of knowing they'll never hurt anyone else ever again." Reese found the spot he was searching for and pulled his car up close to the elevator doors. Slapping it into park, he slipped from the vehicle and Julie punched the redial again. And then he was at her door, so she slipped her hand free of the pocket for the moment. Gun in hand, he made to step up to her right side but Julie moved forward quickly to the elevator and stood to the far right, forcing him to her left side—away from the phone. Her hands found her pockets and she stood there waiting as Reese pressed the button to open the doors. She tried hard not to show anything on her face as she hit the redial button once more.

~~~Chapter Thirty-One

J AMES PACED BACK and forth at the dock. He had just
snapped his cell phone shut on alarming news—news
he'd received from Sylvia—complete with a lack of
pertinent details. Julie was in a car somewhere in the city
with Reese. Any other day that wouldn't have been unusual.
Being James' girlfriend, Julie was often included in down
time with him and his partner. But this wasn't any other day.
This was the day after James had been told that Reese might
be a murderer. He checked his watch uneasily. They should
have been there fifteen minutes ago.

The call of a seagull squawked hauntingly from out of
the light mist. A small flock of the birds drifted and fluttered between ship and water line, calling out to the passengers as though they, too, mourned *The Cormorant*'s human
loss. A car pulled past the security booth and into the gated
parking lot after its driver flashed his credentials and James
immediately recognized Jonas' boyish face. The car pulled
to the curb and ground to a stop. Grabbing his suitcase, he
didn't wait for Jonas' assistance, but yanked open the back

seat door, stuffed the luggage onto the seat and climbed into the front beside the computer technician. "Bring me up to speed. Where are Julie and Reese? Why aren't they here?"

Jonas threw a worried look at him and then swung the car into a u-turn and peeled back out onto the street. "We tried to contact Reese. No answer. So we've been tracking Julie's cell phone for about the past two minutes. I would have called you, but I was almost here. She's one smart lady. She made contact and I'm assuming Reese doesn't know. Steve got a call on his phone—several calls, as a matter of fact. Each time he picked up it was dead air. About the fourth time he jumped on it and had it traced. It was Julie's cell phone and they're tracking it through the city with GPS. I'm supposed to take you back to the office until we know more."

The shrill bleat of a cell phone interrupted Jonas' clipped speech and James fumbled in his jacket for the recently stowed instrument. Steve's voice filled James' ear. "I'm assuming Jonas has told you everything. We've got people heading to an abandoned office complex across town. The signal has stopped there. Are you on your way back to the office?"

"So Jonas says. But Steve, I really want to be there at the scene. I could probably talk some sense into Reese. He'll listen to me." James hoped and prayed that Steve would overlook the emotional connection and just let him do his job—for Julie's sake.

A long pause chewed at the minutes as the car swerved in and out of traffic. "Do it. But send Jonas back here. I need him."

James almost smiled as he dropped the mouthpiece and turned to his driver. "We have a new destination. You're to stop at my place so I can get my car. It's not too far out of the way. Steve wants you to head back to the office, though." Jonas frowned uncertainly. "Just do it, Jonas." He leaned his head back against the headrest to ease the tension building behind his eyes. Hopefully they wouldn't be too late.

"WHERE ARE YOU taking me, Reese?" Julie's voice trembled as they wound down two flights of cement stairs into the bowels of a decaying office building in an abandoned block of similar buildings. It had long ago been vacated by its tenants and it wore a sad, forgotten face. The aging concrete had begun to crumble, leaving portions of reinforcing steel standing out like braces on overlarge teeth. The few windows that hadn't been boarded up were coated with a thick layer of grime. Reese's and Julie's shoes echoed hollowly in the narrow graffiti-covered stairwell.

Reese waved the gun casually, almost as if it were an extension of his hand. "You'll find out. There's someone you need to meet. Now that the ship's docked and I'm a suspect, he'll be just as eager to get out of here as me." They came to the end of the staircase and Reese nodded toward a steel door, indicating that Julie was to open it. The grind of metal on metal announced their entrance into a spacious room, once a basement, now an office. The large desk at the room's center was empty of its occupant, but there was enough evidence to indicate that whoever inhabited the space was an efficient and tidy person. Colourful pictures decorated a brightly painted wall and Julie was surprised by the contrast to the rest of the building. Beyond the desk was a heavy wooden door and it was in that direction that Reese pointed her. "We'll wait in there. He shouldn't be long."

After a curt gesture from her captor, Julie turned the doorknob and pushed the door open to a room that fit in well with the rest of the decaying structure. Walls streaked with grease darkened the effect of the florescent lighting. Scraps of paper and garbage littered the corners of the room. Yet, as in the outer office, the desk was meticulous. Very little covered its battered surface. A small shoe box, lid set neatly aside. A few files. A computer. A telephone. A jar filled with pens. She lowered herself into the worn chair behind the desk and peeked into the box. Across a backdrop of velvet lay military medals. They had been lined up neatly—reverently. She reached out to lift one.

"I wouldn't touch those if I were you." Reese's voice cut into her thoughts, reminding her of her hostage position.

"Why not?" Keep him talking. Keep him busy.

"Nam wouldn't be too happy. They belonged to his dad, who died shortly after the Vietnam War." He hooked a chair with his foot and pulled it close in order to sit.

"So Jeremy Spurgeon *was* behind all of this. And why did you get involved?" Julie took small satisfaction from the surprise that registered.

"So you know about Jeremy?" He dropped his chin to his chest and ruminated over the morsel of information. "Hmm. I guess it doesn't really matter." He lifted his head again as though remembering that he hadn't finished answering her question. "Me? I saw one too many soldiers— our guys—spew out their own guts after ingesting that crap they sprayed on the jungles. I lost too many friends. Good men. Guys like Jeremy's dad. When Jeremy came to me with his idea about getting even, I jumped on it." Julie had seen the file Steve had gathered. A picture of a blonde, blue-eyed boy came to the forefront of her mind. He looked happy as he crowded into the Abrams children. Reese's voice brought her out of the reverie. "Nobody that fights for their country should have to die like that—at the hands of their own superiors."

She could hear the anger and she tried to steer away from it. "What are you going to do with me? I guess I complicate things a bit." It wasn't a topic she really wanted to pursue, but she couldn't think of anything else to say. She swallowed hard against what she guessed was inevitable. And Reese verified her guess.

"Do you really want me to answer that, Julie? If it makes you feel better, I won't sleep good at night after it's over." He sounded convincing. And he was right; it didn't make her feel better.

"Look, Reese. Why don't you just tie me up and leave a note or something? Leave the country—I don't know. Don't make it worse by . . ."

"By what? Killing someone? Julie, we've already killed five people. Do you really think we'll walk away from that with just a slap on the wrist? I'll be facing charges of espionage, assisting in terrorist activity, you name it. Nuts! Killing the General alone makes me a traitor in the eyes of the government. The media isn't going to be kind. And federal prison isn't my idea of a retirement destination. I can disappear for awhile if there are no living witnesses—maybe send for Rita once I'm settled—but Nam—well, he has nothing to pin him down right now. I don't need you showing up and starting a bigger manhunt for him than what's already started. It wouldn't take too much thought for the Bureau to figure out that if they find me, they'll find Nam. And if you live, you could probably help point them in the right direction. Sorry, Julie." His voice sounded weary, as though he just wished it would all be over and behind him. Pinning her with a look, he dropped to a soft whisper. "I will miss you, you know." He looked down at the desk legs and away from Julie's large, frightened eyes.

In the distance a door slammed and both sat forward at the sound. The tread of shoes pounding on concrete grew closer and then the wooden door swung open again.

Julie's eyes grew wide and, for once, she had nothing to say. Reese saw her look and smiled as he leaned back in his chair again. "Hi, Nam. I brought a friend."

"What are you doing here? I don't get it." Julie's shock made her voice sound strangled—stiff.

"Good day, Dr. Holding. I see you've been shown around my little hideaway. Pretty foolish of Reese to do so, but I suppose we can't go back and undo that little faux pas now, can we?"

Reese took on an offended air. "I didn't do it on purpose, Nam. I would be on the dock picking up my partner right now if she hadn't got a phone call from the Bureau chief. I overheard enough. She knows everything. They're looking for you, Nam."

"Really?" The man circled his own desk—including Julie, who was still parked in the chair overlooking the medals. Reaching over her shoulder, he picked up the Gallantry Cross and fingered it as he had done a thousand times before. "Dr. Holding, have you ever seen someone die?"

Julie nodded, keeping her eyes focused on the medal held just above her eye level.

"Hmm . . . I bet you haven't seen them decay, though." It wasn't a question. "It's the strangest thing to watch. The skin seems to be one of the last things to go. It starts inside, and if the victim didn't ooze sweat, you might not know anything was wrong. They can't eat. They hurt. Lumps form under the skin and you know—you just know—that something is eating them alive. They lose weight. They get frail. And then the skin erupts and you literally watch it consume itself."

He set the medal down and turned her chair to face him, pinning her within the shadow of his tall body as he gripped the armrests. "My father stank so bad of rot just before he died that I couldn't even go to him to say goodbye. He lay in his bed and his life oozed out of him. It wasn't much of a funeral; there wasn't much left. All because he trusted a small handful of people in a great big war." Pushing off from the armrests, the man walked around the desk and scooped up the box, tucking it under his arm. Turning to Reese, he looked at the gun and shook his head. "We can't kill her, Reese. She's not one of them. She's an innocent. We can't kill the innocents."

Reese blinked his disbelief. "What do you mean we can't kill her? We have to kill her. She knows who you are. They haven't identified you yet. You could still get away." Julie had stood as Reese spoke, and slowly eased her way away from the chair. The movement caught his eye and he waved the gun at her. "Don't even think about it, Julie."

The man threw a brief glance at her, saw her terror, and shook his head again. "No, Reese. Only the guilty. I don't care about me. I'm not innocent anymore. I haven't been for a long time. Neither are you. But Dr. Holding is. If I'd had a Dr. Holding in my life as a young boy, I might actually have had a life. No, she doesn't die. I have my vengeance."

Anger flashed across the agent's face and he turned an ugly stare on his associate. "Well, I haven't had mine. We could still walk away from this. Julie has to disappear and if you won't do it, I will." Pulling himself from the chair, he made a move to raise the gun. A shot rang out in the cement room, its report pinging a sharp sound off of the heavy walls.

Julie screamed as the body crumpled and dropped to the floor, instantly dead. She would never forget for as long as she lived the sound of Reese's head thumping hard onto the concrete. The man stood there, his own small hand gun hidden within the crease of his large hand. For a moment he stared at the form draped at a strange angle. Thick red liquid stained the floor beneath the still head. Then the man sighed and turned to Julie. Emotionless eyes bored into her and she shuddered at the ease with which the man had just killed his own friend.

～Chapter Thirty-Two

"**D**ON'T EVEN TRY to draw attention to us, Julie," he whispered quietly to her as she prepared to pass through the security gate at the airport. He had smoothly passed the emptied pistol off as her weapon, handing it to her after pocketing the bullets. "All I have to do is grab a security officer's gun and someone will die. It might be you. Or it might be them. I couldn't care less at this point if I live or die, but I'm betting you don't want a death on your conscience, so just play the game and go on through." Julie sighed and nodded, pasting on a smile and pulling her ID from her purse.

The security guard eyed it carefully, noting that, while she worked with the Bureau, Julie wasn't an agent. "I didn't know you guys carried guns too."

She shrugged. "You never know when a patient is going to get aggressive. We take basic self-defence courses too." At least that part was true—she had done it on her own initiative, though. "Look, I'd like to stand here and chat but I'm supposed to be meeting another agent at one of the gates. He's got a guy in custody and they're landing soon. I'm supposed to be there to keep the guy stable if needed. If you want, you can check it out. I'm sure it's in the system. But can you please hurry?"

Handing back her ID, the guard tossed a glance at the long line of people behind her and then nodded for her to pass through.

"Oh, Julie, darling! I've got the ammo in my pocket here. Why don't I put it in with my stuff and I'll see you on the other side." The man offered a wide smile and shrugged an apology.

"You carry her bullets?" The guard frowned and looked from one to the other.

"I don't keep it loaded unless I have to—especially in a public place." Julie felt her face go stiff with yet another life-saving lie. *Lord, please let this man buy this charade. Please spare his life. Take mine if you must, but please don't allow any more innocents to die.*

Her captor had waited for her response, and when she remained silent, he offered a soft smile and drew the guard's attention to himself. "When we're out together, I carry it. Not exactly protocol, but a guy does a lot for the girl he loves." He winked, then, and dropped the shells into a basket. Pulling out his ID and a plane ticket, he made to pass through the metal detector.

"Hey! How come you've got a ticket and she doesn't? Funny coincidence, don't you think?" Subtle suspicion edged the guard's words.

"Not really. I have a flight that just happens to be going out when her guy is coming in. I bought the ticket for this date and time so that I could drive to the airport with her—

a little quality time together in a busy world. Not so unusual if you think about it." The man was smooth. "Why don't you just check out her story and we'll be out of your way?"

The guard tossed another glance at the growing line. He checked his watch and turned to the other guards busy scanning and sorting. The man stepped closer in his moment of inattention and his hand crept toward the guard's sidearm.

Julie could feel the sweat trickling down her spine. Her hands went cold as she watched him move in close to the guard. Stepping forward, she cleared her throat. "Look, sir. You've got a lot of impatient people standing here waiting to get through. Why don't we just go over to a computer terminal and check into the travel manifest for the incoming flight from San Francisco. You'll see the name Special Agent James Benedict and a patient by the name of Perry O'Connell. And you'll probably see a red flag that tells you to expect a Bureau psychologist. Now, can we get that done so this line can get moving?" She stared hard at the guard as he waffled between decisions, then shrugged and stepped aside, allowing the man to proceed. Julie groaned inwardly, unable to believe that they had just pulled off such a crazy stunt. *The guard must be in training or close to retirement. Or maybe he's just having a bad day. Can I relate?* She sighed and moved beyond the security gate. With a few quick strides her unwelcome companion caught up with her and she could hear the amusement in his voice.

"The gun, please, Dr. Holding."

She had forgotten that it was still gripped firmly in her hand and she looked at it stupidly. And then her arm was locked in a firm grip and the weapon was taken from her.

"You have quite an imagination, Julie. Dr. O'Connell wouldn't be too happy to hear that you placed him in forced psychiatric care under James' authority." He discreetly dropped her arm and slipped the gun into his long coat pocket where he worked at reloading it. "Now, let's get moving. It won't take long for that guard to check our stories and then all hell will break loose. I am going to give you my ticket and make certain you are boarded. Sorry about the flight to Miami. I had every intention of taking that flight, but I'll have to make do with my personal jet. I thought a commercial flight would be more discreet, but . . ." he slipped his long coat off, folding it carefully over the gun, then pulled out his cell and barked a few brief orders into it. His pilot would begin the process of firing up the jet.

Snapping the phone shut again, he gripped her arm firmly and steered her toward the gate listed on his ticket. "I appreciate your co-operation in this whole matter—not that you have much choice. Now, let's see if we can repeat the process. They're not going to be too happy about your name not being on the ticket, but we'll see what we can do."

∼∼∼Chapter Thirty-Three

"**M**-M-M-MOMMY! IT'S Miss Julie!" Cassandra's voice piped her excitement and she stabbed a finger at the distant figure striding quickly down the airport's spacious hallway. Before her mother could restrain her, she was up and running toward the object of her attention.

"Cassandra! Hold on! Doctor Holding doesn't need you disrupting her day. Cassandra Carpenter! You come back here!" Mrs. Carpenter huffed as she struggled to catch her daughter. The excited child zigged and zagged through the crowds and would have launched herself at the unaware psychologist except her mother finally caught up, gripping her shoulder and bringing her to a halt.

"Cassandra? What are you doing here?"

Miss Julie didn't smile like she usually did when she saw her small patient and Cassandra hesitated, her excited grin slipping. And then a tall man stepped close to Julie and offered a brief smile and a nod before scanning the crowds. Fear gripped the child's heart. Men weren't always nice.

Sometimes they did things. But Miss Julie wouldn't be with him if he wasn't a good man. Would she? A tentative smile returned and she took a step forward, shrugging her mother's hand aside. Miss Julie shook her head suddenly and the man reached for Cassandra, grabbing her small wrist. The girl screamed once and then shivered as a pool of urine spread across the floor at her feet.

JAMES pulled his car out of the parking lot of the old building. His hands were shaking, his gut churned and he had trouble focusing on the voice cutting through his cell phone. Images floated through his mind of Reese sprawled out on the floor in a pool of blood. He gripped the steering wheel with one hand and steadied the cell phone against his ear with the other.

"Are you going to be ok, James? I know it's a dumb question, but if you'd rather come back to the office, we'll get someone else to track Julie's signal. I already have agents heading in the direction of the airport anyway." Steve was genuinely concerned.

Setting the phone aside briefly, he wiped the back of his hand against his eyes. A horn blared in the background as James ripped through a light changing from yellow to red. He could hear Steve's voice urgently calling him and he scooped the cell phone off the passenger seat. "Yah. I'm here again. I'll be ok. Right now I need to get to Julie. Maybe you can send Jonas on to the airport. I think we'll need extra guys. Steve, he shot Reese right in the head— close range. Whoever this guy is . . ."

"Jonas isn't here, James. I thought he was with you. When he didn't return, I assumed he was there."

James frowned. "No. I sent him back to the office like you said. He should have been there awhile ago. Look, I'm on my way to the airport now. You're sure that's where the signal is?"

"Absolutely. Julie is in the airport and as long as this guy doesn't catch on, we'll track her wherever she is. I'll try raising Jonas." The phone went dead and James tossed it aside and sped off toward the San Diego airport.

SHE COULDN'T BELIEVE the insanity of the situation. Of all the people to be thrown into this kind of chaos and terror, little Cassandra was the last person equipped for it. Julie tossed a brief glance behind her as she raced down the hall ahead of her captor. He ran in close pace with her, the child tucked along with his coat under one arm like a shield to protect him from behind and his small gun pointed at Julie to keep her moving. The Carpenter parents stood in the distance, wailing and pointing at them, and Julie hoped they would be able to get help. Her emotions wavered between uncontrollable fear and anger. If he hadn't seen the security guard walking toward them, she might have been able to keep Cassandra out of it. Instead, he had grabbed the child and shouted for her to run. Like they would ever escape this. *Dear Jesus! Help me to find a solution. Protect us and help James to find us.* The words poured from her soul as she fought to surrender her terror.

Punching the crash bar on the exit that led to the tarmac, the man shouted for Julie to run toward a small aircraft revving up outside a hangar where privately owned jets were kept. Her heart sank at the unbelievable possibility of a jet being there and available for them. *And he probably knows how to fly the stupid thing too.* All chances of escape dwindled as they drew closer to the sleek aircraft. The door was open as though waiting for only them and Julie would have pulled herself into the yawning entrance had it not been for a shout from across the tarmac. She turned to see a gangly bespectacled man running toward them, shouting, and immediately she recognized him.

"Freeze! FBI! Stop!"

The man dropped the girl, gripped Julie by the hair and pulled her in front of him. She could feel the frantic movement of her own heart pounding and gasped as a gun suddenly appeared over her right shoulder. Without warning, he took aim and fired, the blast of the weapon leaving her ear ringing. Julie watched in horror as the agent stumbled, pitched forward and sprawled across the tarmac. Then she was released and shoved back toward the entrance of the plane.

For a brief moment she just stood and gaped, but then a sob caught her attention and she threw a glance at Cassandra, who now sat like a rag doll just behind the man. He stood facing the agent, gun still pointed, and Julie saw her one chance. Grabbing Cassandra's jacket, she dropped to the tarmac, hugged the child close and rolled under the belly of the jet. A blast of hot air from the engine churned the air above her and singed a few strands of hair, and then she was free and up and running, Cassandra still wrapped in her arms. One thought burned in her mind: *Run! Run and don't stop! Get this child to safety.*

"Julie, don't make me come after you." He listened to the roar of the engines and then peeked around the front of the jet. He watched for a brief moment as Julie raced across the runway, the child wrapped in her arms. Blond curls bobbed in a crazy dance against her shoulder. He'd have to be careful to miss the child. He needed a hostage and it was obvious that Julie was no longer willing to co-operate. A deep sigh of resignation burst from his mouth and he raised the gun once again.

A loud pop sounded nearby and Julie recognized the report of a gun. Seconds later, a punch landed on her left shoulder and for a moment everything grew still. And then her legs collapsed and she felt the pain rip through her back. Remembering the child, she twisted to the side, hoping to cushion the impact. The wind was pounded from her lungs and, as black spots swam through her vision, she listened to a distant voice scream her name in child-like tones and felt wet tears drip onto her face.

JAMES COULDN'T BELIEVE Jonas' stupidity. What was the man thinking? With one final burst of energy he sprinted out onto the tarmac, leaving the confusion of the airport terminal behind him. A lot of heads would roll when this all settled. How on earth they got through security was beyond him. The slap of his sneakers marked even strides as he ran toward the jet. What he would do once there, he wasn't sure, but Julie needed him—and now Cassandra—and that was all that mattered.

The bark of a gun shattered the droning hum of a hundred airplane engines revving and dying and he felt his heart jump as he watched Jonas' arms flail against the shimmering air near a small jet. And then the young FBI tech went down, tumbled a few feet and lay still. Beyond him stood a man, his arm outstretched and a gun gripped firmly, and James skidded to a staggering halt as recognition hit him like a wall.

"Sandy? What on earth . . ." And then he was running again, adrenaline pushing him hard. Julie was there behind him and the small child lay crumpled at his feet. James saw it all through the haze of battle frenzy. He watched Julie lean down and grip the child, wrap her in a hug and roll under the jet. He watched Sandy turn at the movement. And then he shuddered, his heart pounding in fear and rage as Sandy calmly dropped his arm, stepped around the front of the jet and took aim once more.

The gun fired at the same moment James barrelled into his old college friend and the weapon popped into the air, breaking free from the pale hand to skitter across the pavement. The hot black surface rushed up to meet the two grappling bodies and the men landed with a heavy thump. James was trained for this and he sucked in air quickly to replace the wind that had been knocked from him. But Sandy hadn't spent all of his years indoors either, and James too quickly found himself fighting for his life.

Chapter Thirty-Four

"MISS JULIE! MISS JULIE! P-P-P-Please wake up!" Cassandra sat against the warm body and wiped at her eyes. There was no response and the red stain on Julie's shoulder was something the child understood all too well. She knew all about blood and the pain associated with it. Her little heart hammered as she tried to think what to do. The fear and torment of her past abuses crashed down on her and she would have curled into a ball and disappeared if she could. She picked up one of Julie's limp hands. It was cold and all she could think to do was snuggle close to keep her warm.

Lifting her mop of rumpled curls, she saw the two men near the plane fighting. One of them looked very familiar to her and instantly her mind flashed back to a shadow in the doorway of a dingy basement. That shadow had moved slowly and quietly, taking off his suit jacket and cooing in gentle words. He had laid his jacket over her shivering form. She remembered him. He had rescued her once before and was now trying to do it again. Tears ran freely as she remembered the day he had brought light back into her dark world. Jesus had used him to free her.

Jesus! Rolling back up onto her knees, she brought Julie's hand with her, lifted blue eyes skyward and stuttered out her heart's anxiety. "J-J-J-Jesus, Miss J-J-J-Julie says you d-d-d-don't like to see children hurt. She s-s-s-says we're all your children. Even the b-b-b-bad people. Jesus, she says you l-l-l-love her and me. Miss Julie needs you to help her l-l-l-l-like you helped me when Mr. D-D-D-Deeder hurt me. Please help Mr. B-B-B-Bena—Bena—help Miss Julie's friend so he can stop this b-b-b-bad man too." She sat for a moment longer, looking at the sky, waiting. A loud grunt drew her attention back to the grappling men and she ducked down to the tarmac once more, wrapped her arms around the unconscious doctor and squeezed her eyes shut tight.

AFTER A FEW last well-aimed punches, both men rolled free, blood dribbling from small, insignificant wounds. Sandy was the first to move, and he scrambled to where his coat lay abandoned. James struggled to his feet to pursue him but stopped short as Sandy whipped around to face him, a glass vial grasped tightly in bruised and battered fingers. Wielding it like a knife, he spread his arms and dropped low. "Come on, James. What's stopping you? Come and arrest me." He smiled. "Unless you already know what I have here."

James threw a frightened look at Julie's still form. He slid his hand behind his back to the holster strapped there. It was empty! Casting his eyes around him, he realized it had worked free and skipped a few feet behind him. Anger surged through his brain. He so badly wanted to grab his gun and shoot Sandy for all the cruel suffering he had caused. It was what he wanted. Vengeance. For Julie's sake. For Cassandra's sake. For all those victims decaying somewhere in the storage units of the morgue. The words of Deuteronomy popped into his head from a Bible study he had been to and James cringed. *It is mine to avenge; I will repay. In due time their foot will slip; their day of disaster is near and their doom rushes upon them.* But he so badly wanted to make the abusers in his world pay now!

"Come on, James. What are you waiting for? If you think I'm afraid to die, you're wrong. I couldn't care less. I have my revenge. Those pigs will never get to hurt anyone else again." Sandy panted hard and took a step to the side. From the other side of the jet came the wail of sirens, voices shouting commands, the clatter of running feet. "You know you want me, James, and I'm going to make it easier for you to decide. You can't get to your girlfriend unless you go through me. And she's dying, so you'd better hurry up." He took another step, planting himself between James and the prostrate form of Julie. Cassandra lay clinging to the still form, her small body shaking uncontrollably.

Dear God! I can't fix this! I need your help! If I have my way, this man will die so he can't hurt anyone again. Help me to trust you.

Peace settled over James and he opened his mouth in surprise and then closed it again. In that brief span of seconds, scene after scene of his own sins flashed through his mind and he remembered Jesus' words to the Pharisees when they condemned a woman for adultery. *If any of you is without sin, let him be the first to throw a stone at her.* Rising from his crouched position, James brought his hands back to his sides. "Just give it up, Sandy—or should I say Jeremy? Vengeance isn't the way." He was amazed at how easily the words slipped from his mouth.

"So I guess you know everything then, huh? How they killed my father with their chemicals? How they killed thousands? How they lied about the effects? I just made sure they got what they deserved. You should be thanking me, James. Your superiors could do the same kind of thing anytime they wanted and you'd never know until you were rotting in your own filth." Sandy was clearly angry and he moved closer. "Come on, James. Kill me. See how good it feels to get even."

James shook his head. "No, Sandy. I'm not going to kill you. As much as I'd sometimes like to see people pay for their cruelty with their lives, it's not right. It's not my way—or God's."

Sandy snorted. "You and your ineffective God! If he was so concerned about people's lives, none of this crap would happen. And don't tell me he didn't plan it this way. I know the whole Garden of Eden story too. And I also know that God didn't do much to help me or my parents when we needed him. You were always trying to tell me God cared—that he loved me. But where was he when my parents died?!"

"He was there, man. He was crying right along with you. He was hurting too because his children were doing horrible things to one another. He's hurting now with you." James held out a hand. "Come on, Sandy. Just let it go. Look. Julie needs help. She didn't hurt anyone. She doesn't deserve to die any more than your parents did. Just let me help her. As you said, you've got your vengeance, so just let it go."

A shout bounced across the tarmac and both men turned to see a half dozen agents with guns raised, calling for Sandy to drop to his knees. James looked back at his college mate just in time to see the small smile and shake of his head. Sandy turned then and bolted toward Julie and Cassandra. James knew instantly that he was planning on using them as hostages and he charged along behind him. Just as Sandy came within five feet, James dove, wrapped his arms around Sandy's knees and pulled him sideways, away from the two bodies. James felt more than saw Sandy drop as his legs folded in on themselves. Reaching out with his arms, the toppling man braced for the impact. A thud, a crack of glass and a curse. And then Sandy was still.

James groaned as he pushed the heavy body off of him and rolled free. The crunch of glass sounded under his side and he turned his head toward the shattered pieces of the hard, clear material. Sitting up, he looked at Sandy and his eyes grew wide. Boils had begun to spread across his throat and Sandy gasped for air like a fish left lying on a ship's deck. James moved closer and rolled his friend onto his side. Parts of the vial protruded from his neck where it had penetrated.

"So how does vengeance feel, James?" The voice croaked its hoarse whisper.

"Sandy, that wasn't vengeance. That was my job. I couldn't let you hurt them. Sandy, I wish things could have been different . . ." James stopped. Sandy was dead. Immediately remembering Julie, he abandoned the body and clambered to his feet. With cautious desperation he shouldered out of his jacket, careful not to touch the bits of damp glass. And then he was off, screaming for help as he scrabbled the remaining distance to her limp form. The several agents that had moved in on the two instantly holstered their service revolvers and scrambled to James' aid. And then the paramedics were there and he was being pulled away.

～Chapter Thirty-Five

J AMES SAT PANTING, his shoulders propped against the step above him. He watched as FBI photographers clicked their way through the crime scene. In front of the jet lay the twisted body of the mastermind whose destruction had cut a wide swath through the men and women of history's shameful past. He could no longer recognize his college pal's face. It must have been a massive dose to work so quickly. Julie was strapped to an ambulance gurney and he watched the attendants work over her. The Carpenters were running across the tarmac to where a second gurney held Cassandra, heavily sedated. He saw it all in a detached sort of way, the adrenaline keeping his emotions at bay while pumping high shots of energy into his veins. Lights flashed, enhancing the bloodstains on the tarmac, and the media stood beyond the security fence snapping pictures and talking into their tape recorders in curt tones.

"You ok?" A shadow fell across him and James looked up, squinting against the flicker of sunlight. Steve dropped a hand to his shoulder and he winced. "You should maybe get that looked at. It's a mighty bad case of road rash."

James nodded. "She going to be ok?" He returned his focus to the paramedics as they hoisted Julie into the ambulance. Pulling himself to his feet, he made to follow.

Steve nodded his reassurance. "Are you sure you don't want to just meet them there?"

"I'm not going to 'just meet them there'!" James snapped and pinned him with an ugly look. "I'm going with her." And then the anger left as quickly as it had come and he offered a weary apology.

Steve nodded and walked along beside James, well aware of the effects of an adrenaline rush. "Who would have thought, huh?" He tossed a glance at the dead body as they skirted past the Center for Disease Control workers in their protective gear and what remained of Jeremy/Sandy.

"He sure had me fooled. I know the blonde hair and blue eyes were a simple fix with contacts and hair dye, but some things I don't get. I thought you said Jeremy Spurgeon was a severe stutterer." James had already begun to seriously doubt his ability to judge character. Two people close enough to him to call him friend, and both were killers.

"I was sure I had told you that Jeremy had gone to speech therapy and it didn't work. Well, it looks like Jeremy was a better actor than anyone thought—and that he had planned his vengeance from a very young age. Ergo the robotic speaking method—part of the therapy." Steve offered a hand as James stepped up into the waiting ambulance. "Look, let me mop things up here and I'll be right over and fill you in on everything."

The doors slammed shut and James shifted to a seat near Julie's head. Her complexion was waxy, but the pulse at her throat still fluttered steadily—a good sign. Reaching out, he gripped her hand. Cold to the touch. He wrapped both hands around it and rubbed it gently to bring some warmth. And as the ambulance bounced and jostled its way through the gate and onto the airport's service road, he closed his eyes and allowed himself to finally relax. It wasn't long before the exhaustion that follows such trauma and the steady movement of the van rocked him into a light doze.

Just as James' head would have dropped to his chest, the blast of the ambulance siren brought him to full alert. Shifting in his seat, he stretched as the vehicle pulled to a stop in the emergency bay.

"Sorry, sir, but you'll have to wait in the emergency waiting room." The paramedic looked at him with sympathy as he swung the back doors wide. "The doctors are going to need to get the bleeding stopped and they don't need someone in the way." And then he was gone, wheeling Julie away from him through doors that shushed open and closed again.

James parked himself at the curb and waited for Steve. He couldn't stand the thought of sitting in the waiting room alone. And he felt more alone than he'd ever felt before. *Jesus, is it true what the Bible says? Is vengeance really God's? Will he really repay it? And how can I let it all go?* He sat there, staring at his feet and listening to the buzz of traffic and the crunch of tires on loose pavement as Steve's car pulled up and parked. The slam of a door and click of heels told him that Steve had seen him, but still, he didn't look up. And then his boss was there, casting his shadow again.

"You ready to go in?" The voice was quiet and concerned and James reached out a hand. Steve gripped it and helped him to his feet.

He sighed and looked at the double doors. What if she died? What, then, of God's justice? Of his vengeance?

"Let it go, James. You did all you could."

"How can you know someone for so long and miss something like this? I've known Sandy since university—and he never stuttered once." James raked his fingers through his hair and fell in beside Steve as they entered the waiting room and sat.

"He mastered a speech technique where each syllable is isolated and over-pronounced. Tone and inflection are removed so the speaker can focus on keeping the vocal chords and throat muscles relaxed." Steve offered a lopsided grin at James' surprised glance. "I called in and asked the same question you did. This is what I was told, which explains why Sandy spoke like a robot. James, I can't help but think you were just part of the whole plan. You knew right out of high school that you wanted to be an agent. I don't imagine you kept that a secret?" James shook his head and looked away.

A muscle danced along the back of his jaw as Steve continued. "A guy's got an FBI agent as a friend. Who's going to suspect him? He faked his own death before he even went to college. Remember? If he knew what he wanted that young you can be sure that he had it all worked out to fool everyone around him. Oh, by the way, as soon as we found out it was Sandy, the Bureau search engine went to work again. We've only got some preliminary information back but would you like to guess who is a majority share-holder in Agrinoram? And in Phelix Corp.?"

James threw a surprised look at Steve. "Sandy?"

"Yes. And I'm guessing that if we look long enough, we'll find the lab where the toxin was made and that lab will have Sandy's fingerprints all over it. I'm pretty certain that if he'd lived to make a confession we would know who killed that Beluga whale all those years back."

A doctor pushed her way through the emergency room door and headed toward James and Steve. Both men stood and waited anxiously.

"Are you family?"

James tossed a brief glance at Steve while the latter was fumbling for his FBI identification and answered, "Almost. I'm about to become her fiancé."

A flicker of a smile appeared and then as quickly disappeared as she gave a brief nod of acknowledgement of Steve's authority. "I've got good news and not-so-good news. The bullet passed through Doctor Holding's shoulder, but it nicked the main artery that runs through her arm. It was very small—thank goodness—or she wouldn't have made it to the hospital. The nurses are prepping her now for surgery. I'm going to go in and repair the artery. Give us a few hours and we'll let you know how it goes." Before James could answer, she was gone and his vigil began.

~~~Chapter Thirty-Six

I N THE STILL quiet a soft whirring could be heard, punctuated by an occasional beep. Julie sighed and stirred as the thick fog in her mind cleared somewhat. A dull ache covered the area between her spine and her left elbow, gradually increasing in intensity until it pinpointed a small area with an occasional sharp pain in the region of her shoulder blade. She winced and opened her eyes to find herself in the pristine confines of a hospital room. Turning her head, she caught sight of a flash of brilliant red on the night stand. Roses. She smiled. The whirring sound became more defined and she dropped her chin as she turned her gaze to the open door on the far side of the room. Someone was running water in the bathroom. A cot separated her from the door to the hall and she knew by the rumpled covers and sheets that it had just been vacated.

"Welcome back to the land of the living." James stood in the doorway in a Bart Simpson T-shirt and a pair of track pants and Julie chuckled at the sight.

"Don't you look casual?" Her voice croaked and ground like the offset gears of an old clock and she struggled to sit up. Pain ripped through her shoulder and she quickly abandoned the idea.

"This is my night wear. I'm not used to sleeping anywhere other than in my own habitat so I didn't think to get something else." Pushing off from the door frame he made a bee-line for the bed and parked himself far enough away to keep from jarring her arm.

"How long have I been out of it?"

"Since yesterday." James lifted her hand and linked his fingers through hers.

A frown shadowed across Julie's face as a thought occurred to her. "Is Cassandra ok?"

James nodded and kept his gaze on his thumb as it stroked the back of her hand. "She's a pretty remarkable little girl. They sedated her for a bit, but when she came to, she wouldn't settle until she could see you. She gave me a hug. Didn't say much. Just a little prayer thanking Jesus for helping you."

Julie blinked away tears, well aware of yet another miracle. The child should have been emotionally devastated. "I'd like to see her as soon as possible. I'd like to thank her for praying for me. I could hear her after I was shot. James, I wish we all had that kind of faith."

"As in 'child-like'? Yah. Me too. I'll give her folks a call and have them bring her in."

"And Sandy? What happened to him? All I remember is running across the tarmac with Cassandra and then falling . . . and her prayer . . . and her hug. I was gone after that." Julie used her good hand to push herself up higher onto the pillow.

James shifted his weight and looked out the window. "It's not pretty."

"Tell me anyway."

"Steve had your signal tracked and we followed it to the office complex. What made you think of it?"

Julie smiled and shrugged a shoulder. "I saw it on a movie." The smile disappeared as quickly as it had come and another memory hit her hard. "Reese!"

"Reese." James sighed. "I don't know how he managed to keep so much from me. And Sandy too. Am I that bad at judging character?" James asked the question, not expecting an answer.

He got one anyway. "You picked me. Doesn't that count for something?"

Julie's smile returned and James countered it with his own. "I guess I did more than ok with that one." Another pass of his thumb across her hand brought silence, and then James finished what Julie didn't know. "Jonas got hit. Sandy—Jeremy—hit him in the leg. He'll be ok, though. I got to the airport too late, but at least it was easy to find you. When I saw you go down I thought my world had ended. I went berserk and charged Jeremy."

"He actually does a pretty good tackle." Steve's voice cut across the room and both turned to see him standing in the partially opened door. "Is this a private party or can I join?" He pulled a bouquet of daisies from behind his back and held it out as though to bribe.

Julie laughed. "Please join us. You can help fill me in on what I missed."

"It's pretty simple. James knocked Jeremy down and rescued the fair damsels in distress. What a nasty way to go, though. He got a taste of his own medicine—quite literally. He must have taken on a whole vial of the stuff. There's not much left of him."

Julie reached out and stroked James' cheek, trying hard with the gesture to consol him of such a huge and irreparable loss.

Turning his head, he planted a kiss on the palm of her hand and sighed again. "No one should have to die that way."

"I'm so sorry, James." She dropped her hand to his.

James tried to shrug it off as best he could, knowing that a time of mourning would come. "It's one of those choices people make." He turned to his boss, who still hovered in the doorway and offered a wan smile. "Why don't you come in and sit down, Steve? You don't have to stand out in the hall."

Steve looked from Julie to James and chuckled. "I think I'll come back after you two get the mushy stuff looked after." With that, the door whispered shut again.

Julie stared at the door for a moment and then turned a curious look to the quiet agent. "And what mushy stuff would Steve be talking about?"

James inched closer and dropped a gentle kiss on her bruised forehead. "He's probably talking about the part where I give you this. I got it on board ship." He leaned over and grabbed his jeans off the cot. Riffling through a front pocket, James withdrew a small black ring box and flipped it open. A diamond flashed from its cradle of black velvet and Julie's eyes welled up.

"Yes." Her voice broke with emotion.

"I guess that answers a question I never got to ask. But that's ok with me. For now, you need to get better. We have some serious plans to make." James slipped the ring on her finger and rose, planting a last soft kiss on her lips.

Bibliography

Federal Bureau of Investigations website. www.fbi.gov.

Hozey, Kevin and Brian Ashbaugh, eds. *World History and Cultures in Christian Perspective 2nd edition*. FA: A Beka Book, 1997. http:// www.abeka.com.

People's Daily Online. http://www.english.people.com.

U.S. Marine website. http://www.marines.com.

U.S. Military website. http://www.military.com.

Vets With A Mission. http://www.vwam.com.

Wikipedia: The Free Encyclopedia. en.wikipedia.org

More from Donna Dawson

Redeemed

ISBN #1-894928-75-X
Word Alive Press, 2006

Heather never intended to harm her family; it wasn't in her nature to do so. But when her temper began to take control of her life, she feared for the safety of those she loved.

After viciously attacking her younger sister, Heather takes matters into her own hands and runs away from home, hiding in the parks and streets of Toronto. It is in that overlooked and unwelcome part of society that she finds a new family, a ragtag group of vagrants who take her in and teach her about loyalty and survival—about who to trust and who not to.

When she ends up in the clutches of a warped club owner, it is these friends who come to her rescue, delivering her to a multi-denominational soup kitchen where Heather comes face-to-face with her failings and the One who is greater than even the destructive power that drives her.

Will Heather be able to escape her past? Will she be able to begin a new life? Or will she be forever bound in a world of corruption, deprivation and loneliness?

More from Donna Dawson

Adam & Eve Project

ISBN #1-897373-01-5
Word Alive Press, 2006

Conflict rages across the world as Hitler vies for global dominance. One by one, European countries fall to his brilliant military schemes. The free nations watch like a wary creature watches a predator and, while all eyes are focused on the conflagration, children are mysteriously disappearing.

The Adam and Eve Project will take you through government intrigue, murder and suspense, human manipulation and the ultimate freedom— salvation.

Upcoming Novels

Rescued
Fires of Fury
Vampire